A View of The Bridge

A Novel by Chaka Adams

PrettyGirlsRead

www.PrettyGirlsRead.com

Published by PrettyGirlsRead™, LLC
Cover Art © 2012 by PrettyGirlsRead all rights reserved
Cover Layout & Design – HotBookCovers.com
ISBN 978-0-9887010-5-2
First Printing January 2013
Printed in the United States of America

PrettyGirlsRead
Atlanta, GA
www.PrettyGirlsRead.com

Dedicated to Mommy and Daddy
My love eternally...

My Siblings – Stephanie, Gina, Bo, Raheem, Tineeka,
Shekia, Khaseem, Rahman...

Madison and My ROCK forever...

Johnnie Monroe & Pat Gallo - thanks for inspiring me

With Love to Ms. Yvette Cushnie in memory of Kyra

And to Shakeena, Samlith, and Denise
Without whom, none of this would be possible

FOR QUEENSBRIDGE...

PREFACE

When I first wrote this book, I didn't think to add a preface. In my eyes I felt the words and messages contained within its pages would suffice. Funny thing I learned through becoming an author is that many authors are full of shit. But it wasn't until I started receiving feedback from my fellow "authors" that this gem was dropped on me like a boulder.

I was advised to add some plot twists to give the book a 'WOW' factor. No really, like I should have told y'all that the reason my life was so fucked up was because as I got older I realized my biological mother had sold me to a pimp and the mother I thought I knew was really a former mule for the Columbian Drug Cartel or was it the Italian Mafia from Little Italy? That shit was so stupid that I can't even remember which one it was.

And oh yeah, another one of those twists included adding that my brother was plotting to kill me because he owed money for a gambling debt to some ruthless Russian immigrants who owned the local casino down the Atlantic City strip.

And because I wasn't confident as a writer, with this being my first novel and shit, I figured I'd start the first chapter with a shootout in the middle of a Federal Court House. I would be blazing through the metal detectors to free my Miami drug kingpin boyfriend so that we could escape on our private jet to a secluded unchartered island in the south of France. And my dumb ass thought, yeah, let me add those never-happening-in-true-life shenanigans and then maybe, just maybe, my book will sell.

FUCK OUTTA HERE... If you're looking for that type of book, then by all means, please bring this one back to the register and demand a refund. This is not that type of book.

Believe me, I wasn't flying in private jets. Actually, I still haven't flown it one yet but you better believe I'll be Mile-High Clubbing it very soon (I kid, I joke, I digress). But anyway, I thought about it and I accepted the fact that I wasn't going to sell-out. I write for the streets and I come straight from my heart. My words reflect who I was at the time in which I felt the need to grab a pen. I'm comfortable in my own skin and it has taken years for me to be able to say that.

Lest we forget, I'm a Gates Millennium Scholar who graduated with honors from a highly accredited university. I'm far from dumb. And my readers are far from dumb – they know bullshit when they read it. Integrity is everything.

So, with that being said, I chose not listen to the editor who told me, I'm a pretty girl who should be writing "pretty" books. I'll continue to ignore the self-righteous bourgeois agent who advised me to create a Hollywood-themed setting in order to attract a "different type" of reader. If I have to be fake in order to sell books, well then maybe I won't make much of a profit with this one.

This book was conceived from reading through journals I've had over the many years. As I look back on the person I was then, I'm amazed at how much I've grown. Every step I made in life has been a result of my own choices and the many opportunities I missed simply because I didn't know they existed - *especially not for a girl like me.*

I hope this book will act as a deterrent for some and as a source of closure for others. For both, let me say, you're not alone. I have been where you are or where you were. The only difference is that one day I woke up and said, "I'm worth so much more."

Hopefully, while reading this book, you will understand why I didn't sell-out. You will respect my authenticity and agree with me for keeping it completely transparent. And because I did, there will be at least one person who will grow from my story. And in the end, that's all that matters to me.

Prologue

I don't even know where to begin. It seems as though so much has gone on in my life that I can barely recall how it all started. It's like reaching a point where everything around you seems to stay in the same fucked up predicament while only you have managed to change. I feel like I'm the one crab who actually made it out of the barrel. And if you've ever seen a barrel of crabs, you know what I'm talking about.

Every time one gets close enough to the top, there's another fucking crab tugging at its legs bringing it back down to the bottom. Some crabs never make it out. They just die, never leaving the barrel at all. Dead crabs make it twice as hard because all their dead weight, dead dreams, dead hopes lie on top of the motivated crab and suffocate its optimism.

Well, that's where I am in life right now – a fucking crab, just struggling to stay out of the barrel.

The gossip hounds are still sitting on the same project benches they've been sitting on for years. The faces may change but the conversation never does.

"Yeah, you know that ain't even his damn baby," says one.

Quickly followed by the other, *"Well the police just ran up in Yvonne's house the other night looking for her son."*

If you've ever lived in the hood, you are very well aware of just who the gossip hounds are and probably have played the role yourself a time or two. They're never happy unless they have a story to tell.

Then there's the niggas on the block selling everything - crack, weed, heroin, cocaine - you name it, they got it. Of course the ones sitting on the block ain't shit but small timers selling drugs to get money for sneakers, weed and pussy. They're the simple ass niggas that get locked up for a bullshit six to nine months bid and come home like they were a King Pin or something. Those are the dudes that would shoot their guns in a crowd and hope they get the nigga they wanted to hit. More than likely, they'd miss their target and hit some innocent bystander or some stupid shit like that. They don't ever have shit except a bunch of baby mamas all living in the same hood.

And, let's not forget about the baby mamas, the young loves, jump-offs, mamis, cokehead cutie pies, gold diggers, chickens, pigeons, smuts – yeah, by any name they use, they're all up in the hood. A project chick is unlike any other chick in the world. She's the mother and foundation of the black family, yet in the same breath, she's more trifling and conniving than a strung out dopefiend. She's the best friend that will fuck your man and also the chick that would happily set that same nigga up to get robbed. But when the police come around she's the first one to step up and take the weight just to keep her other nigga from going down.

She's the mother that can take her last three dollars and make a feast with a dollar worth of chop meat and a ninety-nine cent box of no-frills white rice. If she budgets her money wisely, she'll still have enough to cop a twenty-five cent pack of Kool-Aid, a pack of Drakes Butter Crunch cookies for dessert and of course have enough left over for a fifty cent loose cigarette from the corner bodega in the morning.

Donald Goines said it best when he called her a *"Black Girl Lost"* because she truly is lost. She's lost in her own web of deceit and treachery. Her pussy is her weapon but her heart is her downfall. I know because I am her or should I say I've been her...

And here's my story...

CHAPTER 1

QUEENSBRIDGE, 1993
"Chaka, yo Chaka"

The call was coming from the street corner up to my fourth floor project window.

"Chaka, tell them fast ass girls that we have a phone now so they don't need to be calling you out my window like that," my mother yelled from the living room.

I thought to myself that it made no sense to waste a quarter on the public pay phone outside when calling me from the window would work just as well. The intercom downstairs was always broken anyway so how else would they get me to come out? Besides, we would need those quarters to buy Phillies later on.

But to appease my mother, I yelled to my friends that I'd be down in a minute. I could barely see them through the small opening of the metal bars on my window. The bars were New York City Housing's idea of keeping us little black kids safe. I mean, with all the random shooting and drug wars going on outside, at least we didn't have to worry about falling out of the project window. I wished my mother would have gotten those things taken off. There were no more kids in that house, especially not me. Shit, I was sixteen and looked about twenty.

I checked myself out in the full length mirror behind my

bedroom door. The room was so small that I practically had to stand on the bed just to get a head-to-toe look.

"Damn, I look good," I said to myself.

My long black hair was pulled back into a French roll and neatly held in place with nearly a whole jar of gel and at least fifty hairpins. I never really got into that make-up phase. My mother always said black girls were naturally beautiful and didn't need all that make-up plastered on. She claimed it took away from God's masterpiece. So, a little Vaseline rubbed on my lips was all the sparkle I needed.

My pink Tommy Hilfiger t-shirt worked well with my cinnamon complexion. I thought it was a blessing to be light-skinned because whenever I was with my friends, who came in every shade of brown imaginable, guys would always holler at me. I guess I just had it like that.

My mother was dark-skinned and got teased about it throughout her childhood. I think she consciously had kids with light-skinned men so we wouldn't have to go through the same thing but she would never admit it and believe me, I asked.

My Portuguese father gave me my complexion. At least he gave me something I could use to my advantage.

I tightened the straps on my bra so I could appear to have bigger breasts. I thought about stuffing them to give me a little extra *oomph* but I figured against it. I was definitely a member of the itty-bitty tittie committee and proud of it. Besides, more than a mouthful was a waste. Even though, I really didn't have enough for a mouthful and nobody was putting them in their mouths - at least not yet anyway.

I wrapped my hands around my size two waist and did a full turn. As I did, my new white Nike tennis skirt also did a complete swirl with me. The skirt was short enough to emphasize my long shapely legs. All the old-timers in the projects would always tell me I had my momma's legs - thick, firm and perfectly shaped. Well, what I lacked in breasts, I sure made up for in legs and a cute little ass.

I looked down and noticed a scuff mark on my brand new pink Air Max sneakers. Hurriedly, I rushed to the bathroom and got out the toothbrush to wipe them off. I paid over a hundred dollars for those sneakers and I was damned if I would mess them up. Actually, I didn't pay a dime of my own money but I had to flirt long enough with some young nigga for him to cough up the dough. When my mother asked me where I got the money from for the sneakers, I made up some lie about finding a wallet with cash in it. She must have believed me because she never said anything else about it.

"Chaka, you better go downstairs before them girls start calling you out my damn window and I have to curse their little grown asses out," my mother yelled again to my bedroom.

She must have forgotten that I was supposed to be on punishment for coming in late the night before. Here I thought I would have to beg to go outside and she was practically pushing me out the door.

"Dag Ma, all right, I'm going," I whined, while making my way into the living room.

The living room was small just like the rest of the apartment. My mother had wood paneling on the walls. It made her feel like we didn't actually live in the projects. The couch and love seat were beige which she made sure stayed that color by smothering them in plastic. I hated sitting on the mummified furniture because in the summer I would burn up and stick to the seat. Then, in the winter, the plastic was always cold regardless of how many blankets I used. If I made one move on the couch, the loud squeaks echoed throughout every room of the apartment. Maybe the plastic was her way of hearing every move that was made in apartment 4A.

My mother was watching television from her usual spot on the couch near the window. She was one of the few women in the hood who actually had a job. But on her days off, she was a typical couch potato. Of course her favorite show was on, *The People's Court.*

"All right Ma, I'm going out. Love you." I kissed her on the cheek and tried to rush out the door before she remembered my punishment.

"Oh and Missy, don't be coming in my house all hours of the night either. You better check in by ten o'clock."

"Mommy, ten o'clock? Come on, none of my friends even have to check in anymore." I was salty as fuck about being the only teenager who still had a curfew.

"First of all, I'm not their mothers, I'm yours. And I don't care if they don't want them to check in. You will, period. And don't think I forgot that your butt is supposed to be on punishment. Today is a test." She threw me that 'Black Mama Look' which silently let me know she meant business.

"What punishment? You must be thinking of your other daughter. I never get in trouble." I planted another kiss smack dab on her lips. Only that time, I flashed her with my baby girl smile.

"Yeah, yeah, whatever Missy. You better check in by eleven and I mean that. Try me if you want."

I knew she'd give in. She was always a sucker for my gap-toothed ass.

"Good looking Mommy. See you at twelve - love you."

In a rush to get outside, I grabbed my keys, which were sitting in their usual spot on top of the entertainment center.

"Girl don't make me come out there and have to look for you 'cuz you know I will. Twelve o'clock and baby," my mother paused, "I love you too."

As I walked out of the apartment, I was relieved she let me off punishment. That was the first hot day of the year and I knew for a fact that everybody who was anybody would be outside. When the weatherman said it would be eighty-four degrees, I ran right to Steinway Street to cop me an outfit. Since it was only a five dollar cab ride from the projects, it was sort of like the hood's Mecca for clothes. Everybody shopped there.

I decided to walk down the four flights of stairs because I was looking and smelling too good to ride in our pissy-ass elevator. No matter how much they tried to clean it, it would still stink like stale urine mixed with cheap industrial strength ammonia. I definitely didn't want that stench clinging to my new clothes.

When I emerged from my building, the sounds of the projects hit me all at once. Radios were blaring from opened apartment windows. Tires screeched loudly as cars sped along the busy intersection not giving a fuck about the stop signs or the little old ladies trying to push their shopping carts across the street. Snotty nosed kids were running all around, jumping in and out of the fenced-off dilapidated grassy areas which were randomly mixed in among the concrete.

People didn't have to leave the hood for any reason whatsoever. We had a clinic, a beauty salon, a church, a grocery store, a barbershop and of course a liquor store that was right next door to a rat infested Chinese restaurant where we never knew if it was actually chicken we got with our order or the homeless cat from down the street. There was even a Queensbridge library which most kids stopped going to once they reached the age of ten.

Mostly everyone I knew had a mother or father who was born and raised right there in Queensbridge. It was like a never ending cycle. In fact, my family was still living in the same apartment my mother lived in since the day she was born. The same streets that were raising me, had once raised my mother. My bedroom used to be her bedroom. My grandmother's bedroom had become my mother's bedroom. It's just like that in the projects. Because apartments can be handed down from one generation to the next, people rarely made it out and didn't have much of a reason to even try.

At the end of the day, Queensbridge was really all I knew. And since the projects only had six blocks, which held exactly ninety-six buildings, everybody knew everything about everybody else.

My friends, Sheena, Reece and Kia were all sitting on the wooden benches in front of my building. They also had on their best outfits for the first hot day of the year.

"Damn girl, we was just about to leave you." Sheena whined as usual. "Shoot, what took you so long?"

She stood up as I approached. Surely she was trying to show off her yellow High Top Reeboks, which we called Fifty-Four-Elevens because that's how much they cost in the store with taxes and everything. They were exactly fifty-four dollars and eleven cents. She would have almost looked decent if she didn't have on the same pair of white spandex leggings she always wore whenever we would try to get cute. No matter how fly we pretended to be, Sheena accessorized every outfit with a pair of spandex. And she didn't just have the basic black pair. Sheena had all different flavors – polka dot, striped and airbrushed. Of course spandex didn't cost as much as a pair of jeans so she could afford to buy a whole wardrobe worth of them. She was cute, a little on the heavy side though. But like me, she was light-skinned so she always stood out from the crowd.

"You know y'all wasn't even gonna leave me. Anyway, I was getting ready." As I was trying to explain what took me so long, I caught Reece looking me up and down from the corner of my eye.

I never really liked Reece and I'm certain the feeling was mutual. But, she was the most popular one out of all of us so I just hung around her. Although, I still don't know what her intentions were for hanging out with me. Maybe I was the flunky she needed to make herself feel better about her own fucked up life.

Her brother was a local drug dealer so she always had the latest sneakers and designer clothes. She wasn't cute but she dressed nice and since her parents were in jail, she pretty much got to do whatever she wanted. She lived with her brother but he was always in the streets so he never cared about what she was doing as long as he didn't have to watch her.

Regardless of how much she spent on getting her hair done, she had that type of shit that just wouldn't grow. She was constantly getting micros from the African braid shops in Harlem. Sometimes, I forgot what she actually looked like without her Yaky ponytail. That bitch kept a horse's ass freezing just to get a head of synthetic hair.

"How much money you got?" Reece asked me with her snide ass tone of voice.

"My mother gave me five dollars before I came outside. What's the deal?"

Kia, the tomboy of the bunch grabbed the money quicker than I could even get it all the way out of my pocket. "We all gonna put in five and get a dime from the Dreds, a six pack of Heinekens and a box of Newports. And I heard we should use White Owls instead of Phillies because they burn longer."

Leave it to Kia to know all the latest developments on the weed scene. I had known her since elementary school but we didn't hang out much until that summer. She was always fighting and getting in trouble so people rarely bothered with her. She was only like five feet tall but she could fight her ass off and had the stitches from getting her face sliced to prove it.

"Chaka, you go to the Dred and get the weed," Reece demanded. "He likes you so he'll give us a fat bag."

I didn't care that she was practically ordering me around because the truth was that the Dred always gave us a lot of weed whenever I went to buy it. The bigger the bag, the more weed to smoke. So it was pretty much a no-brainer, I was the designated weed-copper.

The Dred was in a convenience store across the street from my building. On the outside it looked like the typical bodega but everything inside the store was more than five months past the expiration date. Nobody ever bought anything from in there but I guess the police never noticed the lack of grocery bags in the hands of customers coming out. More than likely, they simply just didn't give a fuck.

"So give me the money and Sheena, you coming with me. I ain't going in there by myself." I grabbed her arm right before she could stuff that last piece of Lil' Debbie Honey Bun into her mouth.

"Damn," I thought to myself, *"how could she already have the munchies and we ain't even smoke yet?"*

"Ay, there pretty gal, what's up?" Dred spoke to us from behind the bulletproof glass.

He was tall and slinky looking with a long dreadlocked ponytail that hung down his back nearly touching his ass. His skin was so dark that when he smiled all you could see was a mouth full of tarnished gold teeth. In true Jamaican fashion, his clothes were mismatched with every loud color of the rainbow. Nobody knew his real name so we just called him Dred.

"Hi Dred," I replied with a little flirtation.

"Ay gal, when ya gon' let me take ya out and show ya a real nice time, heh?"

The harassment was becoming a routine with him. I would have found weed from somewhere else if his shit wasn't so good. I guess degradation had to accompany the hustle.

"Come on Dred, I'm too young for you and you already

know that." I wished Sheena would have pulled herself away from the stale bags of chips on the wall to interrupt us.

"Yeah me know how old ya is," he snickered. "Man, what me want wit' a ole dried up gal when me got a juicy little gal like you right here, heh?"

I rolled my eyes, completely frustrated with the shit I had to endure just to get some good bud. I slid the two five dollar bills through the slot and demanded a big bag. Shit, if I had to listen to his crap, the least he could do was look out for me on the weed tip. He reached under the counter and pulled out a dime that looked more like a fifty dollar bag. To my surprise he didn't take my money. As I reached for the bag he grabbed my hand instead.

"Ya keep ya money. Pay me another way, hah. I mean another time."

I pulled my hand away from his grip but not before I snatched up the ten dollars and bag of weed.

"Here." I slipped Sheena a five dollar bill as we were about to leave the store. "And don't tell them he gave it to us for free either."

I had to hip her to the game before she ran out and blabbed that we had gotten the weed for free. If I didn't, then we would have all had to split my little profit and I was having none of that. What Reece and Kia didn't know wouldn't hurt them.

"Let me see the bag," Kia said, not even giving us enough time to completely walk out of the door.

"*Damn,*" I thought, "*talk about thirsty. She could have waited until we were all the way out of the store first.*"

"How much did he charge y'all?" Reece asked.

"How much you think? Ten dollars." Sheena was quick to respond while throwing me a side-eye that only she and I noticed.

While we were in the store getting the weed, Reece and Kia had already gotten the beer and cigarettes. Unfortunately, the bodega didn't have White Owls but none of us really had a problem smoking the weed out of a Phillie since that was the only thing we were used to back then.

Our only problem was finding somewhere to sit and get our smoke on. Usually we'd pick any bench we wanted and sit right outside. But that day was a little different because the weather brought everybody out. And bringing everybody out basically meant the gossip hounds would make sure that word got back to our mothers about us smoking weed.

With no other options, we decided to go to the River Park which was secluded and at the very end of the projects. Beyond the river was a clear, almost photographic view of Manhattan. There we were, broke ass ghetto chicks from the hood staring across the blackened East River into million dollar condos. It would almost make you forget you were still in the projects. That was until you looked around and found the little drug baggies and 40-ounce beer bottles thrown all over the ground.

Kia was in charge of rolling the blunt because she did it the best out of all of us. Perhaps it was her gangster persona that enhanced her ability but the bitch had her technique down pact. First, she'd crack the Phillie open right down the middle and dump all the tobacco out. The prissy chicks would use a razor but we were from the streets so we split that shit apart with our own bare hands. She'd then dump the bag of weed into the Phillie paper and take out all the seeds and branches. Only trash weed had a lot of garbage like that so since we got weed from the Dred, we didn't have to waste much time doing that shit.

Then she'd break up the weed in between her fingers. The stickier it was, the better it tasted and the higher we got. After spreading the weed along the Phillie paper, the next thing she would do was grab it at both ends and roll upwards. Then came the part where you couldn't allow just any foul-mouthed person to roll the weed. In order to close the Phillie, Kia had to lick the paper until it stuck together.

PERFECT! Her blunts made you just want to sit back and analyze the shit for a while before smoking it.

We sat in a circle, which we referred to as a cypher. Who knew what that word really meant but it sounded good so we used it. The unspoken rule was two pulls on the blunt and pass. Yet after you start talking and smoking, that rule is quickly forgotten.

"Y'all know it's a basketball game on Tenth Street today right?" Sheena managed to speak between chokes from the weed.

By my count she was already on her fourth pull.

"Yo Sheena, pass that! What you doing, baby-sitting the shit?" Kia was obviously keeping count as well.

"We should go y'all. I bet there'll be mad niggas there," I said, after taking a few swigs of my beer. In those days it only took one Heineken to get me tipsy.

I really wanted to go to the game. I knew I had on a cute outfit that day and needed to flaunt it. It was always a thing with me to be in the limelight. Although I fronted like I ignored the little snide remarks that guys would make about me, the truth was that I loved the attention. My dream was to have a baby by the biggest drug dealer in the projects and become his main lady. After I had his baby, I knew Housing would give me my own apartment. I wouldn't even have to work because my man would be making money and I could get welfare for my little extra pocket change. I had my future mapped out completely.

Once I got my apartment in Queensbridge, my man would undoubtedly lace the crib with leather furniture, a big screen TV and even get me some vertical blinds. I would find some crackhead with good carpentry skills to build me a wooden platform in the dining room so it would feel like I had an upstairs and downstairs. My baby would have all the cutest GAP clothes, the newest Jordans and I would be pushing a shiny red Aprica stroller. I even had their names already confirmed. If it was a boy, I'd name him Saquan or Shakim. My daughter would have to have a classy sounding name such as Mercedes or Madison, like the avenue in Manhattan where all the rich white people shopped.

Everybody would respect me because I was the lady of the biggest man in the projects. I'd be that chick that all the little girls wanted to be like and all the older girls wanted to befriend. It was a plan for the ultimate ghetto paradise, and at that age, I didn't want for anything more.

"What you thinking about over there, girl?" Sheena asked, interrupting my daydream.

Damn, weed used to have me tripping sometimes.

"Nothing. Come on y'all the weed is gone, let's be out."

We gathered our beers and walked toward the basketball court. And trust me, basketball wasn't the only game that was about to be played.

CHAPTER 2

The music blaring from the speakers at the game hit us way before we reached the basketball court. As Nas' song, *"The World Is Yours"*, pumped from the DJ table, we found a spot on the crowded block where not only could we see everything but everybody could see us as well.

The teams were playing wearing t-shirts with either a number 12 or a 10 printed on the front to represent their blocks. Ain't nothing like a fine ass nigga playing ball on a hot sunny day. What was even sexier was the way they would lift up their shirts halfway, exposing their sexy abs, to wipe the sweat off their foreheads. Those were the good guys, the ones who got accepted to all the private high schools to play ball. They didn't smoke weed and were never in the drug game. Needless to say, I wasn't attracted to those types of guys at all. I needed a thug in my life, somebody that everyone in the hood knew and thoroughly respected.

There were three main cliques of girls, at least as far as my generation was concerned. And yes, they were all at the game. There was the gangsta bitches clique, who was always stumbling through the blocks, drunk from drinking cheap ass St. Ides beer. Not a night went by in the hood without those chicks getting bent and fighting somebody. They were, as my mother liked to call them, a bunch of tack-heads. Only the dirty ass broke niggas were really feeling them. Their popularity came as a result of their ability to fuck a bitch up in a New York minute.

Now the other clique was more on our level. They were classier than the gangsta bitches and had clout with the moneymaking niggas like we did. In fact, all of us would hang out and chill together at times. However, it was always on some fake ass shit because as soon as they would leave and it was just us again, Reece and Kia would talk about them like dogs. I looked over the court and saw one of the girls from that clique approaching.

"Oh brother, look at that bitch coming over here," Reece said out of the corner of her mouth.

Before she had a chance to get the words completely out, she was already talking out of the other side of her face. "What up girl? We was just about to walk over there and say hi."

"Oh well," I thought, *"let the fakeness begin."*

"Y'all all fucked up and shit. Look at your eyes. Y'all need to light it up, fa' real," Ta-Ta, who was the youngest and wildest of that clique, yelled.

I swear that girl didn't know the meaning of using her 'inside voice' if her life depended on it.

"Yeah, we just had a session at the park." Sheena chomped on an egg roll that somehow miraculously appeared in her hand.

I didn't even know where she got it from because we never stopped at the Chinese restaurant. Sometimes I thought she was stashing food in her bra or something. I was still shocked she didn't admit that we had gotten the bag for free. I guess she appreciated that extra five dollars just like I did. I'm sure she would use it to get something else to eat with her fat ass.

"Ta-Ta, them shoes is banging! Where did you get them?" Kia asked.

"Oh these ain't nothing, you know how I crush 'em. I got them the other day from this Italian boutique on Steinway." She did a little jingle of her ankle as she bragged, confident and cocky as usual.

Ta-Ta never gave a fuck about what anybody thought. I always liked that about her. She was who she was and whoever didn't like it - oh well, it was their problem and not hers.

"Yo, it's half-time. Y'all go to the store, get ya smoke on and do whatever you gotta do but be right back here to see the two illest teams in the hood go at it."

The voice coming out the speakers was Corey's. Now that nigga was who I needed in my life. His respect ran so deep that people referred to him as the Mayor. He was the head of the Enforcers who were an infamous group of older dudes who had the streets on lock. If any young buck wanted to pump drugs on a block, he had to go through them for permission. Believe you me, they were getting a cut off the top.

We were way younger than the Enforcers but that never stopped them from going at us. Any girl who could bag one of them niggas and settle down would be set for life. Everybody in the hood would go out of their way to speak to her and look out for her all the time.

Since I was so young, they wouldn't consider me to be one of their ladies. I was still in the 'young love' age bracket. But in the hood, everybody wanted a young love, especially a P.Y.T. - pretty young thang. That's why the older chicks hated us young girls. They knew we were one menstrual cycle away from taking their men. Hey, they shouldn't have hated the players, they should have hated the game. I'm sure they did the same thing when they were coming up so it was only right for them to eventually reap what they sowed.

"Hi Corey," I practically yelled across the court.

Shit, I was going to make sure somebody was flirting with me. I looked too cute to go unnoticed.

Corey heard me and walked over. Even his walk was sexy. He was tall and husky like a football player. His cornrows were spinning all around his head like Allen Iverson's but he still had it shaped up around the edges. When he spoke, my pussy would start to throb at the sound of his voice. He had a harsh and rugged tone that made me want to strip naked for him right there on the spot.

"Y'all enjoying the game?" He asked.

"Nah, forget the game, I came to see you." My words were

heavily coated with flirtation.

"Yeah, all right," Corey chuckled, sounding more like a pedophile as I think back on it now, "you about to get your little ass in trouble. You ain't ready for all this."

He grabbed the bulge in his pants as he walked back to the DJ table. He laughed it off but not before looking me up and down. I knew he was checking out my legs.

"Ayo, you crazy," Ta-Ta blurted out loud with a slap on my back. "And I heard that nigga got a big dick."

We all laughed but I was imagining just how big it really was. At that point, I was ready to lose my virginity. I had waited until I was sixteen, which was a lot older than most of the chicks in Queensbridge. I was a woman who needed to be deflowered. And I wanted Corey to be the one to do it.

"So what y'all getting into tonight?" Ta-Ta asked.

"I don't know, probably nothing." Reece hurried to answer for all of us.

"Well come on our block later. We'll be at the card table." She walked back toward her clique, who was only a bench or two away from us.

"Yeah right, we ain't going on that weak ass block with them." Kia made sure she waited just long enough for Ta-Ta to be out of hearing distance before she started with the phony shit.

"Puhleeze, I know that. I just wanted her to leave," Reece chimed in with a laugh. "And did you see those shoes?"

"She ain't get them from no boutique on Steinway. I just saw those cheap ass shoes in Easy Pickens the other day."

Now since Kia was the tomboy out of the bunch I doubted she knew anything about shoes anyway. Instead of worrying about somebody else, she should have been shopping for something other than the same dirty Guess jeans with black rings around the pockets that she wore every Monday, Wednesday, Friday and twice on Sunday.

For my part, I never indulged in their petty gossip sessions. I actually liked those girls and they never did anything to me for me to talk about them. Honestly, gossiping was never my twist. My mother always told me that loose lips sink ships so I learned early on in life how to shut the fuck up.

"Malik," Sheena called out.

I didn't want to look but I could sense that he was standing right behind me. Malik was one of the Enforcers but he was too ugly to get any of my attention. He would always ask about me which made me sick to my stomach. He was about five-two, give or take a few inches, skinny, black as shit and his teeth were all fucked up. Instead of two front teeth, he had like ten which all seemed to be fighting for room in his mouth. He met my standards in every other capacity. He had money, respect, a nice car and everybody knew who he was. But in my opinion, he looked like the toucan from the Fruit Loops cereal box.

"What up?" Malik's voice squeaked like a key scraping against a chalkboard. Everything he did turned me off.

"Hey Malik!" Reece and Kia addressed him in unison like a god-damn choir.

I was pissed that Sheena had called him over, knowing full well that I couldn't stand him. She must have felt guilty about it because she didn't bother to look my way.

"Chako," Malik snickered, while tugging at my skirt.

Without even looking at him, I responded with the illest attitude I could muster up. "My name is Chaka, not Chako, for the millionth time."

I don't know why he would always call me that as if his little nickname for me would change the fact that I threw up in my mouth a little bit every time I looked at him.

"I know your name. I just like to see you get mad. Why don't y'all take a ride with me after the game?"

Reece quickly agreed. "Aight, we'll meet you on the Ave when it's over."

"Bet and make sure you bring Chako with you." Malik pointed back at me as he walked off.

"No, don't even ask, I ain't going nowhere with that nigga."

"What you mean you ain't going?" Kia asked.

"Y'all could go but I'm not."

I couldn't believe I had to explain myself to them. The mere thought of him disgusted me. They knew I couldn't stand his ugly ass but still, they were trying to force me to go.

"You gotta go, Chaka. The only reason why he wants us to

go is so he could see you." Sheena finally looked at me while munching on a Twix.

Who knew where she got that from?

Her comment didn't make me change my mind. If anything, it only re-emphasized my initial decision not to go.

"Chaka, come on," Reece coaxed, sweetly laying down her game. "It ain't like we gonna be with him all night. We'll take a ride with him then get him to go to One-Two-One for some weed and we'll be out. I promise."

For some reason or another, I could never say no to that broad. She had a way of talking me into everything and my dumb ass would do it just in order to be her friend.

"Yeah well, I have to be back at twelve so I'm not staying with him all night either."

I knew not going would be pointless since I'd just be left in the projects by myself while they went with him anyway. I didn't want to be stuck in the hood walking around with nothing to do after the game was over and everybody went about their separate ways. Besides, One-Two-One, which got its name because it was located on 121st Street in Jamaica, Queens, had the best weed. Their shit was even better than Dred's.

"We'll be back by then," Reece assured me. "Come on, let's walk around."

We made our way through the packed basketball court stopping here and there to bullshit with everybody.

"Damn, y'all gonna be the future clique out here." For a grown ass man, Rashawn always lacked tact as he glued his eyes to our asses switching across the court.

Rashawn was older and down with the Enforcers. He was a muscular sexy-chocolate type of nigga but he was broker than a mother on welfare with five or six kids. We called him Broke Ass Ra amongst ourselves because he was always walking around fronting like he had mad money but was repeatedly asking somebody for a dollar. He would act like he just happened to run out of change but we all knew he was broke. I mean, come on, how many times per day could somebody run out of change?

"Yeah, watch out for them, they gonna be hurting something when they get older," Corey added.

He gave me that look that let me know he was ready to personally show me the statutory truth behind those big dick rumors floating around about him.

All the Enforcers were sitting on the bench by the DJ table. I was glad we finally made our way over there because I wanted to pick up exactly where Corey and I had left off and hopefully move on to the next level.

"Chaka," a familiar voice called out from behind.

I turned to see Jamere standing there with a smile that automatically made me smile right back. Quickly, I reached up to give him a hug. He lifted me off the ground and squeezed me close to his body.

"Come on Ja, I got on a skirt stupid," I yelled loudly as he placed me back on the ground.

Out of all the guys in the hood, Jamere was the only one who never came at me on some sex shit. When I was younger, I used to skip school to sit on the bench with him for hours keeping him company and watching out for police while he sold his drugs. For my part, he would hit me off with a couple of dollars whenever I needed it or treat me to breakfast at the little Spanish restaurant across the street from my block. But the truth was, I liked being around him so much that I would have done it for free anyway. He was down with the Enforcers but I looked at him more as a big brother than a potential sponsor.

He was tall and built like a basketball player. His athletic body worked well with his curly hair and light brown eyes. He must have had Indian or Puerto Rican in his family because his complexion was like a smooth piece of caramel they sell at the penny candy store. He was gorgeous but his sense of humor made him appear more like a friend instead of a boyfriend. I was in love with him, that much I'd admit, but it was never in a sexual way. He was my friend, nothing more and nothing less. People always spread rumors that we were messing around but it never happened. I knew better than to get involved with somebody like him because relationships always have a tendency to fuck a friendship up with the quickness.

"What you doing with that short skirt on anyway?" Jamere playfully slapped me on the top of my French roll.

"Come on Ja, you gonna mess up my hair." I patted my edges to make sure nothing was out of place.

"Mess up your hair? That bun is so hard I almost cut my damn hand."

"It's not a bun, it's a roll. And it's hard because I use gel. If your bald-headed lady had hair, then you would know what it was." My comeback was witty and quick and that's what Jamere loved about me. I was just as sarcastic as him and could definitely hold my own in a game of verbal chess.

Reece, disturbed that I was the center of attention, was ready to go. She yelled loud enough for everybody on the bench to hear.

"Chaka, come on. You gotta meet Malik on the Ave. He's waiting for you."

"Now why did she have to say that shit out loud?" I cursed to myself, not wanting anybody to know I was going to see him of all people.

I shot her an evil eye to let her know she was dead wrong but she pretended not to notice.

"Malik?" Jamere was obviously shocked.

I knew hanging out with Malik wouldn't sit too well with him but that was his friend so he stayed neutral. At least that was his reaction while we were in front of everybody else.

"Yeah, but I'll be right back. See you later."

I quickly turned away so he wouldn't have time to respond. However, I wasn't quick enough.

"Chak," Jamere called out as we were walking away.

I stopped and waited as I let the girls go ahead. The last letter 'a' in Chaka must have taken too much energy for some people to say because they always broke my name down to one syllable and simply called me Chak. I took it as a term of endearment, so I never corrected them.

"Yo man, watch that cat." Jamere's usual nonchalant nature had disappeared.

"Oh, he's just taking us to get some weed, that's it. You know you my Boo." My gap-toothed smile was front and center, hoping it would give Jamere some reassurance.

"You heard what I said. And yeah, you mine too."

When he walked away, I turned and noticed the girls had already gotten to Malik's car. Hesitantly I made my way toward the Ave. I figured one day with *"Toucan Sam"* wouldn't hurt. But no matter what, I had no intentions on letting him touch me.

CHAPTER 3

"**C**hako, what took you so long?" Malik asked before I reached the car.

"I was just minding my own business, something you obviously know nothing about." I immediately cut his possessive streak short.

If he thought we were going to have an enjoyable booty-call car ride, he was surely in for a rude awakening. Reece tried to laugh my comment off and told Malik I was just playing. She knew I was dead serious but wanted to make sure he would still take us to get some weed. And like the manipulative bitch she was, she knew how to spin it so that he wouldn't think twice about the slick response that came out of my mouth.

As if they already had it planned, Reece, Kia and Sheena all jumped in the back seat of Malik's rented Toyota Camry.

"One of y'all get in the front and let me sit in the back," I demanded, holding onto the car door expecting somebody to trade places with me.

"Nah, we already sitting back here. Just sit up there and stop acting like that." Kia grabbed the door from my hand and slammed it shut.

Sometimes I look back and wonder how my life would have turned out had I not gotten into the car that day.

"Come on Chako, I don't bite." Malik's smile was big enough to show all two hundred of his front teeth.

With that grill, I was lucky he didn't.

Reluctantly I got into the front seat as Malik sped off toward the highway. We merged onto the Van Wyck Expressway where there was nothing but four lanes of cars speeding, swerving and dipping across lanes. He was doing about ninety miles per hour and driving like a bat out of hell. Tupac's, "*I Get Around*", was playing on the radio while the sun roof was opened just enough for the highway air to flow freely on our heads. I was glad the music was turned all the way up so I wouldn't have to talk to him during our trip.

"Malik, the police are behind us," Kia warned.

Checking his rearview mirror, he reached into his pocket and pulled out a small brown paper bag, which he placed on my lap. "Chak, hold this."

I grabbed the bag and without asking any questions, I stuck it up my skirt and into my panties. Maybe it was the speed of the car, which casually began to slow down, but my body was full of adrenaline. I felt like I was on some Bonnie and Clyde type of shit. God knows how much drugs I was holding while my man, I mean, while Malik was driving to escape the police. If I knew exactly what an orgasm was back then, I probably would have had one.

See, if you're not from the hood, then I don't expect you to understand the rush I felt. In fact, you're probably wondering why I'd willingly accept the drugs Malik threw into my lap. Maybe if I was from the suburbs or someplace like that, I would have gotten all scared and panicked. But I was from the streets, I had to represent. There was no other choice but to show Malik and my friends in the back seat that I could hold my own.

"Stop looking through your mirror. They can see you doing that," Malik said. "If we get pulled over, I don't have no license."

I could have smacked myself after hearing his admission.

That meant if the cops stopped us, they would have definitely made us all get out of the car. We would have probably gotten searched and the only one that would have gone down, would have been my dumb ass. Somehow, I always managed to get myself in the most fucked up situations.

I felt the police pull up next to us, slow down and look over through the passenger side window. My heartbeat quickened as we all tried to keep from turning toward them. It felt like an eternity before they decided to drive up and pass us. As they did, the whole car let out sighs of relief – the loudest one coming from me.

Malik was a lot smarter than I had originally thought. He knew he was dirty with drugs in the car. He also knew the police were less likely to stop a car full of girls than a car full of black goons. So his intent on taking us for a ride had less to do with getting with me and more to do with us being his mules helping to transport his shit. Immediately, I liked him a little bit more for his street smarts if nothing else.

After the police drove away, I didn't bother giving the paper bag back to Malik. The truth was, holding the drugs in the crotch of my panties actually made me feel important. I thought about my so-called friends in the back seat and wondered how they felt about Malik not thinking they were down enough to hold his shit. He trusted me and I came through. They were just flunkies.

We finally exited the highway and pulled into the Edgemere Housing Projects in Far Rockaway which was at the very end of Queens. Because it was way out there, it seemed like it should have been part of Long Island instead of one of the city's five boroughs. I hated that place for many reasons – one, because my mother's best friend was killed there years before and secondly, because that was the place New York City Housing sent people who were too ratchet to live in the inner city projects. Far Rockaway was just far enough away from the city that real New Yorkers never had to deal with the people out there or their trifling ways.

When we got out of the car, I was impressed with how everybody knew Malik. As random people walked by, they stopped and shook his hand or gave a silent nod of the head as a form of hello. It says a lot about somebody when they get respect from another man's hood. I started to think that perhaps Malik wasn't so bad after all.

"Chak, come with me and y'all stay in the car."

Malik singled me out again from my clique and I liked that. I looked back at them with a feeling of superiority as he and I approached his friends in front of one of the project buildings.

"This here is my young love, Chaka."

As Malik introduced me, I didn't mind my newfound label because with that title came respect.

"You got any friends that look like you?" One of the guys asked.

"Almost," Malik said, with a sense of pride.

I cracked a smile, thinking I could definitely get used to that sort of attention.

As we entered the house, I was expecting to walk into a typical crackhouse - busted furniture, dirty people lying around the floor, a refrigerator with nothing in it but an old milk bottle filled with tap water. But the apartment we entered was far different than what I had imagined. It had all the amenities of a condo on Park Avenue. There was a stainless-steel microwave, plush carpet, air conditioning, nice furniture - whoever lived there had to have a little bit of money. Come to find out the apartment belonged to the girlfriend of one of Malik's friends. Ironically, she was a Corrections Officer on Riker's Island, the city's most over-populated prison. I figured that had to be the best place a young chick could work because she would get to meet drug dealers from all the hoods across New York City.

Malik caught me off guard as I was checking out the apartment. He reached under my skirt and grabbed the bag of drugs while slipping me a quick kiss on the cheek. Usually, I would have flipped on him for doing that but for some reason or another, I kind of liked it. As he walked into the bedroom with the other guy, I sat on the tiger-print chaise and scoped the place out.

While waiting, I noticed there were pictures of the girl and her baby scattered all over the entertainment center. Her man wasn't in any of the pictures and her child looked like he was damn-near white so I suspected Malik's friend wasn't the baby's daddy.

The girl was all right looking and that was putting it nicely. She was a little bit lighter than me with long box braid extensions that hung down her back. She had on some nice clothes and crazy jewelry. Her ring, which she made sure was visible in every picture, was the biggest diamond I had ever seen in my life. I immediately began to imagine myself in her place. She didn't look half as good as me and if she could get all of that stuff, I knew I wouldn't have any problems getting a nigga to foot my bills. It was at that moment that I realized what I wanted and who I was going to choose to get it for me.

"Chak, you ready?" Malik asked as he stepped out of the bedroom accompanied by his friend.

I looked at him and surprisingly, he didn't seem so facially-challenged anymore. In fact, for some reason I figured the combination of both of our genes could possibly make some all right looking kids.

Yes, I know I was moving a little too fast. But on the streets, there's only one way to move and that's faster than two shakes of a lamb's tail. If you move too slowly, you just might miss something.

The day went a lot smoother after that. We all rode down the elevator in complete silence. My head was too full of thinking about what color towels I wanted to put in my bathroom than to hold a conversation. As we left the building and walked to the car, my friends were looking at me with their faces all screwed up with envy. There I was, taking care of business and they had to sit there and just wait until I was done.

"Y'all ready? Let's go to Jamaica to get y'all some weed." Malik finally acknowledged the real reason we came for the ride in the first place.

We all piled back into his car. Only, I didn't mind sitting in the front seat. Shit, I wouldn't have sat in the back if somebody asked me. Fuck that, I was the HBIC - Head Bitch in Charge, and it was definitely time to act like it.

That was the day I crossed over and became a product of my hood. Actually, that was the first day of the rest of my life.

CHAPTER 4

"Sheena, let's walk down to the store on the Ave."
I was sick and tired of sitting on the benches in front of the beauty parlor with absolutely nothing else better to do.

"For what? It's one right there, Chaka," she replied, pointing to the candy store directly across the street.

"Come on, I go with you everywhere."

"I ain't even about to be walking way down there. You just wanna see Malik anyway and we already checked - he ain't down there!"

As many times as I had walked her somewhere to stalk a random uninterested-in-her ass nigga, I couldn't believe she wouldn't walk me right down the block. She should have wanted to go because Lord knows she needed the exercise. Instead, she only budged to stuff her fat ass hand into a bag of crunchy Wise Cheez Doodles.

"WHATEVER!" I stomped away in a rage. "I'll go by myself."

It had been a week since making that run to Far Rockaway with Malik and I hadn't seen him since then. His disappearing act was unusual because he used to always manage to track me down when checking for him was the furthest thing from my mind.

While making my way to the Ave, I started thinking that he should have been sweating me instead of the other way around.

Maybe he thought I wasn't interested so he just moved on. No, there was no way I was about to let that happen. I couldn't let another chick get the life I felt was rightfully mine. If I had anything to do with it, I'd never go back to sitting in the back seat looking like a loser.

I knew I had to show him what I was all about and make him start hounding me again so I could wrap him around my little finger. I felt important that day in Far Rockaway and I wasn't ready to give that feeling up for anything in the world.

Malik's car pulled up to the corner just as I had gotten there. Unfortunately, he had his bum ass lady Erika with him. Finally, I had a chance to holler and he was with her tired looking ass.

Erika could have been cute. In fact, she was a dime back in the days. But three kids and allegedly four baby fathers later, she just looked like a washed up had-been. I had never muttered as much as a hello to her so I didn't feel any type of way about scheming on getting with her man. Besides, Erika was a joke. She never had a job, she wasn't classy and with all the money Malik was making, she always managed to look broke. I don't even think she got her hair done on a regular basis. But she did have the one thing that could tie any nigga down in the hood and that was her own apartment. The best way to keep a man, especially when he doesn't have any place else to go, is by giving him a spot to lay his head.

I thought about turning around and walking back to Sheena but they had already seen me. I decided that I was just going to walk right by them and head into the store across the street, that way I wouldn't be so obvious. I expected Malik to act like he didn't notice me as I strolled by but to my surprise he called out to me as he and Erika got out of the car.

"Chaka, my man wanted me to give you a message."

I was almost speechless at the audacity he displayed by trying to get at me in front of his lady like that.

The emphasis being on 'almost speechless' for I was truly never one without words.

"Oh, really? Well, tell your man he don't got nothing to say to me after a week done went by." I knew for damn sure that he was the one with the message.

If he was going to disrespect his lady, I would too. After all, she didn't mean a damn thing to me. I wasn't the one who had to go home to her every night.

Malik turned to Erika and whispered something low enough so I couldn't hear. Even though I was unable to make out the words, I knew whatever he said had pissed her off. If looks could kill, I surely would've been dead right then and there. She gave me a serious ice grill which let me know that she knew I was after her man. But hey, it was just bad karma on her part. She took her man from another chick and now I would take him from her. That's the way it goes. If you live by the game then it's only a matter of time before you lose your man to another woman's game.

I cracked a smile at Erika in a rubbing it in sort of way. All she could do, in her defense, was stand there and pitifully roll her eyes. After forcing his lady to reluctantly walk away, Malik began to lay his game down on some real pimp type shit.

"Chak, what's up?"

"What you mean what's up? You act like you can't speak to nobody no more." I was trying to sound like I had an attitude but I knew it wasn't working.

Pretending to be mad was a waste of time because when our eyes met, I couldn't help but smile. He was wearing a black Army certified jacket with matching pants. His Timberlands were fresh black suede without a visible scuff even though it had been raining all day. The sparkle from his diamond flooded watch kept poking out from under his sleeves every time he moved his hands. I watched him closely, never blinking an eye.

"Well, you acted like you wasn't interested so I decided to give you some space, you know. I just chilled," he said.

Damn, what did I do wrong?

I wanted him to be interested so I knew I had to recapture his attention somehow. He probably smelled my naivety a mile away because he started really spitting some heavy shit.

"Look, I'm twenty-nine years old Chak, you know what I mean. I'm a grown ass man and I ain't got time to be playing these little girl games with you, fa' real. If you about it, then be about it and stop wasting my time. But you know what, that's on you. I can't make you do a damn thing."

I was taken aback for a minute but then I placed my hand on my hip and put a twist in my neck before responding. "First of all, I'm not a little girl and I don't play no little girl games. I'm grown."

I was offended that he had the nerve to call me a little girl of all things. In my infantile brain, that was the biggest insult.

"Yeah, that sounds good but I ain't with all that talking. I'm about to go up to my spot. You can come up there and kick it with me if you want, I mean, since you ain't no little girl. I'm going up there now so you come in about five minutes. You know the building right? Its apartment 6F."

He walked away without even looking back. He must have known I was going to follow him just like a lovesick puppy.

I stood there for a second, trying to really understand how the conversation had managed to flip. He was supposed to be scheming to get with me but somehow he turned it the other way around. I guess all the cards were on the table and I either had to play or fold. Now, I'm not a poker player but I knew enough to know the person who folds is quickly eliminated. And since I was not about to be discarded, I figured I would just have to play the hand I was dealt and see how it worked out.

The five minutes felt like five hours but I was finally making my way to his building. The door wasn't locked which was a good thing because I didn't want to be spotted waiting outside for someone to open it. I walked into the coffin-sized elevator where the sound of my pulsating heart echoed throughout. It finally stopped and I hesitated before getting out. The 6F on the apartment stood out like a neon light and I was drawn to it like a moth to a flame. I stopped and just stood there, too afraid to move. I wanted to run off but since I had gotten that far, it made no sense to turn back around.

Fuck it, it's now or never.

A lump formed in my throat as I began to knock softly on the door. I almost jumped out of my skin from the sounds coming from the other side. Malik opened up, giving me full view of his vicious looking Rottweiler chained to a pipe in the kitchen. He grew more excited as I walked further into the apartment. As his mouth salivated, I kept looking at the chain around his neck knowing if he pulled on it any harder he would break away from the pipe and I would be history.

"Don't be scared, that's just Bandit. Stand back while I shut him up."

The name definitely didn't fit the crazed lunatic dog that continued to lunge toward me. I thought Killer or Cujo would have been more fitting. Malik grabbed a muzzle from off of the floor and placed it tightly around Bandit's jaw. Needless to say, I still didn't feel any safer.

A look around the apartment left me extremely disappointed. It was so much different than the one we visited in Far Rockaway. There was only one couch in the living room that had stuffing coming out of the ripped holes. The battered old wooden card table was in the dining room with two lop-sided metal folding chairs around it. No, it was not the paradise I had previously envisioned. I didn't bother to check but it's likely the refrigerator only contained an old empty milk bottle filled with tap water.

Malik held my hand as I hastily walked by Bandit and into the bedroom, which looked as bad as the rest of the apartment. There was a twin-size mattress thrown on a rusty bed frame. I almost tripped over the many boxes filled with clothes and papers that were scattered around the floor. The lamp in the room didn't work so we had to leave the door open to use the light coming in from the hallway.

I sat on the bed and waited for Malik to say something. God knows that I was too nervous to open my mouth. But instead of talking, he just started kissing me. I didn't mind though, I knew I had popped a piece of Juicy Fruit in my mouth so my breath was fresh. His kisses became more aggressive as his breathing intensified. He started pulling at my hair, which fell long down my back. The harder he kissed, the harder I kissed. I wasn't as excited as he seemed to be getting. I mean, damn, I had gone so far as kissing before. However, I did try to mimic his moaning sounds to let him know I was feeling him as much as he was obviously feeling me.

I felt his hand begin to unbutton my jeans. He struggled before actually getting them opened. I was glad he got it because I felt too paralyzed to move. He laid me down and started to grind his hardening dick against my leg. Part of me wanted to tell him to slow down but part of me knew this was what I had to do to get him to want me again. He slid his finger gently inside of me.

"Oh shit, your pussy is so wet and tight, damn." Malik groaned, as he pumped deeper and faster into me.

I had done the finger-popping thing plenty of times, so that was nothing new. In fact humping wasn't new to me either. I had been humping since junior high but for some reason, being with Malik felt different. I had never gone that far with a real man before.

He grabbed my hand, shoved it into his pants and rubbed it along his dick. "You feel that? That's you."

I didn't know how to respond. I mean, was that supposed to make me proud or something? There I was, lying on a twin size mattress, getting finger-popped, while holding a dick in my hand. I had no idea what to do with that thing. I had never even been that close to a real dick in the flesh. Was I supposed to rub it? I mean, should I have squeezed it or something? I didn't know what was supposed to happen next. After all, I was still a virgin.

"Go ahead, play with it," Malik whispered into my ear as he guided my hand from the shaft near his balls up to the head.

My moves on his dick were robotic - up and down, up and down. There were so many thoughts occupying my head, that I couldn't concentrate on the right way to rub a cock, if there was a right way anyway.

Besides, I had more important things on my mind, like the thing every woman thinks about before she's about to get busy, "*Damn...what panties am I wearing? Are they sexy or are they Granny's panties?*"

I was in luck. I remembered I had on my silky flowered

bikinis that I got on sale at Conway's – five pairs for ten dollars.

He started to pull my pants down toward my ankles. I was still motionless. I wanted to tell him that I was a virgin but everything was happening too fast for me to get the words out of my mouth. I felt him jam his dick into my body. The swiftness of his movement caught me off guard forcing me to bite my bottom lip to stop from screaming.

"Damn yo, you a virgin?" Malik continued to thrust himself deeper inside of me.

"No," I managed to shriek through the pain, "I did it before."

The tears welled up in my eyes and Malik continued humping as if I wasn't even in the same room. I couldn't believe that all my friends said sex felt so good because I felt like I was being ripped apart from the inside out.

To escape the pain, I closed my eyes and imagined I was somewhere else. I pictured the ideal place that I always dreamed of losing my virginity - king size bed, candles burning, rose petals, champagne, Luther Vandross singing in the background and a lover that was soft and gentle. Instead, I was getting deflowered in an abandoned, roach-infested crackhouse. I was glad the light in the room was broken because I didn't want Malik to see the tears that poured from my eyes.

After he pumped for a few minutes, totally oblivious to my existence, he started making some strange grunting noises. His face got distorted and beads of sweat began to leap from his body.

"What's wrong?" I was scared as hell. He looked as if he was having a seizure or something.

"Oh shit, I'm about to cum."

As his thrusts grew more intense, he grabbed my shoulders and pulled me so close that his dick felt like it was in my stomach. My moans got louder but they weren't moans of pleasure regardless of how hard I tried to make them sound like they were. They were moans of excruciating pain.

"AGGHHH," Malik screamed aloud before his body collapsed on top of mine.

His chest was wet and sweaty. The only sound was coming from his heart, which seemed to be beating a thousand times per minute. We laid in complete silence for a few seconds until I heard a strange noise.

What the fuck? Is this nigga really snoring?

I couldn't believe that after all that, there was no caressing, no bed talk, no I love you. Instead, he just passed out with his dick still inside of me.

"Malik." I tapped his shoulder lightly to awaken him.

"Yo, Chak, that shit was some good shit."

He finally sat up and looked at me. My hair was all over the place from being constantly pulled. I managed to hold back my tears of disappointment. Disappointment in Malik, disappointment in my choice of places to lose my flower, but most importantly I was disappointed in myself. Deep down, I knew I deserved better. But then a part of me wanted to believe that eventually it would get better than that.

Malik got up without saying a word and jumped into the shower. He wasn't even romantic enough to ask me to join him. I wanted so badly to get up, get dressed and get out. However, I was not about to walk into the living room by myself, with that crazy mutt. Besides, I wanted to talk to Malik. I wondered how he felt about me since I had clearly proven I wasn't a little girl.

He came out of the bathroom with just a towel wrapped around his skinny dark-skinned waist. I watched him walk across the room and giggled thinking about how hideous he looked when he was cuming. I bet if he knew what busting a nut made him look like, he would think twice about fucking half the chicks he fucked.

"So now what?" I asked, in an attempt to finally break the uncomfortable silence.

"Now what, what?"

"You still think I'm a little girl?"

"Nah, Chak you definitely ain't no little girl that's for damn sure. But check this out, I gotta go meet somebody so get dressed, aight."

I couldn't believe he was practically throwing me out the door after I had given him my most prized possession. I dressed quickly, feeling both ashamed and rejected. Before I knew it, he was fully clothed and waiting for me as if I was taking too long to get out.

He wrote his beeper number down on a piece of paper and handed it to me as he walked toward the door. He didn't have the decency to walk me downstairs. He made me leave first and then left five minutes after so people wouldn't think we were together.

Before he closed the door, I turned around in hopes that he would at least give me a kiss. He pretended not to notice the puckering up of my lips. Instead, he just stood there trying to gaze off in any direction other than looking into my eyes, which at that moment, yearned for even the smallest hint of acceptance.

As I left the apartment, I left behind an important part of me that I would never regain. I entered apartment 6F as a naïve and trusting little girl. But the person walking out of that door was a whole new Chaka altogether.

CHAPTER 5

I wanted to run home, lock myself in the room and cry. Leaving Malik's apartment was the ultimate walk of shame. My head hung low, so I wouldn't have to look anybody in the eye. As I darted through the block, I felt a sharp pain shoot through my abdomen which stopped me dead in my tracks for a second. Not wanting to draw any attention to myself, I took a long deep breath and despite the intense cramps, I continued on my way home. I could see my building from where I was but it felt like the closer I got to it, the further away it became.

Once I got inside, I didn't bother waiting for the elevator. Instead, I ran all the way upstairs. My tears were uncontrollable as were my legs which dashed right beyond my apartment on the fourth floor and up to my cousin Taylor's crib just one flight up. I knocked on her door and prayed for her to be home. As soon as she opened up, I ran into her arms and let the sobs roll. My body flinched every time I let out a groan.

"Chaka, what's the matter?" My cousin questioned me while rubbing my back in her attempts to calm me down.

I felt so comfortable in her arms that it was hard to pull away and tell her what happened. My words were tangled within my cries but somehow I knew she'd understand. Barely making it all the way into her apartment, I blurted out the events that had just transpired with Malik.

"Is that it?" Taylor asked. "That ain't nothing. You're just growing up sweetie, that's all."

My cousin led me toward the bathroom and grabbed a towel from the linen closet. She ran the water in the shower and assured me that I would feel better once I got in. I didn't want to let her go as she finally released herself from my grasp and closed the bathroom door. I got undressed and saw spots of blood on my panties and streams of it sliding down my leg. When I finally entered the hot shower, I let the water pour all over my face. I gently scrubbed my swollen vagina for what felt like an eternity trying to clean away any part of Malik. When I finally decided to get out, I cringed. Of course I wasn't feeling any cleaner than when I had gotten in.

Taylor had put some sweats and a t-shirt in the bathroom for me to change into. I pulled my hair, which at that point was wet and curly, into a ponytail with a random scrunchy that was lying around the bathroom. Finally, I emerged and felt somewhat decent again.

My cousin Taylor had been through it all. She was about ten years older than me and was more like a big sister. In fact, we weren't really blood related but our families were so close that calling each other friends just didn't seem fitting.

Taylor was the baddest bitch in the hood back in her prime. She had a baby by the biggest drug dealer in Queensbridge during the 80's, when that crack epidemic had the hood looking like a scene from *The Walking Dead*. She was the only role model I had ever known. Her hazel eyes and light skin were instant focal points for all the money making niggas around the way. Her mother put her in private schools so she was smart and classy as well – perfect combination.

When I was younger, I would babysit her son and pretend he was mine. I was like her shadow, always under her, always watching, always learning. She definitely showed me how to appreciate drug money by taking me shopping, out to the movies and even getting my nails done.

Being a part of her world back then when her man was on top was so much fun. She taught me all the flashiness of being a drug dealer's lady. Her closets were filled with mink coats and butter soft leather jackets. Even though she didn't know how to drive, her dude bought her an Alpha Romero car that stayed parked in front of the building. Taylor rose from being just another Pretty Young Thang to being the top chick in the projects. Unfortunately, shit changed once her man went to jail.

Her baby's father, Supreme, caught a drug charge and had to do a ten year bid. When he left, Taylor's ghetto infamy went right along with him. Bitches no longer respected her and niggas were no longer intimidated by fear of her man. Taylor became just another average chick on the streets. All her groupie friends simply moved on to the next chick on top who took her place. Not me though, I stuck right by her side through it all. Besides, after seeing her go through what she endured, I was determined to never let that happen to me.

One thing I can say about Taylor is that her fall from grace was full of class and dignity. She never asked anybody for a dime and never let the next bitch know if she was struggling or not. I respected her for that among everything else.

She listened intently as I babbled about every detail, from the first ride to Far Rockaway to the way in which he kicked me out of his apartment. She didn't interrupt nor could she with the rate of the words coming out of my mouth per second. I couldn't shut up. Yet, when I was done confessing my transformation into womanhood, I sat back on her bed and prepared myself for a good schooling. I wasn't the least bit disappointed with what Taylor had to say.

"Well, first of all, throw his number away. He gave you some dick now he expects you to sweat him. I'll be honest with you Chaka, Malik is the last person out here that you should've given some ass because he's a dog. But you did it and you can't change that shit now."

She was right, I couldn't change the past so I had to move on and play the game. She told me to be patient and wait for him to come sniffing back around like a dog in heat. I could almost guarantee that he had never had pussy as tight as mine so I was sure he would have wanted more. Erika was all old and dried up with stretch marks and a black hole where her pussy should have been. She didn't have anything on me.

In all reality, probably right this very minute, while you're reading the words in this book, some young girl is somewhere losing her innocence in a foul environment just like I did. It's just like that in the hood. Taylor said all ghetto superstars had to start somewhere. Since she was once the biggest superstar, there had to be some truth to her words. So, my only choice was to trust her and stay optimistic.

Taylor and I talked for about an hour before I felt comfortable enough to face my parents. As I turned the lock on my apartment door, I took a long deep breath before going inside. My mother and father were on the couch watching television as usual. By father, I mean my step-father, although I never referred to him as such. That man had been my Daddy since I was eight months old. He stepped in and took the next man's responsibility, which is a lot more than I can say for the average black man in the ghetto.

I looked at the both of them and was so proud at how much they had changed. From as far back as I could remember, my parents were both heroin addicts. I heard that back in the 60's, shooting dope was just like smoking weed – everybody did it. Unfortunately, dope was far more addictive and resulted in dire consequences for so many from that generation.

But it was because of them, that I had a love for the streets. In order to support their habit, they created a good con-team. Usually, my brothers and I would tag along to be used as an extra twist to finagle people out of their money. It just so happened that I was more intrigued than my brothers who found it difficult to get into character. Not me though. Even as a child, I loved hustling. It was my chance to be someone else. We'd go to people's houses and pretend I was selling something for school. I'm not sure how my mother would scheme her marks while we were in there but I knew we would always leave with enough money for them to get high and for my brothers and I to have McDonald's.

Of course some would say my parents were unfit and just plain wrong for involving their kids in a part-time hustle. However, I disagree with those sentiments. They were well aware of the impact it would have on us throughout our lives.

By bringing us along, they were merely teaching us how to survive. Sure, a college education can take you far but there's no education like the school of the streets. When white people go broke, they jump out of windows or off of a roof – some dumb shit like that. Yet when black people go broke, we depend on a hustle to get by. Regardless of how hard shit gets, we learn at an early age, how to survive.

But as time went on, my parents left the streets alone and slowly but surely the drugs were left alone with it. My mother even started going to church which was a stretch for her because I remember her wild days when she would curse the pastor out for knocking on our door. We went from sitting on plastic milk crates to sitting on plush couches. As my mother always said, God works in mysterious ways.

I went straight into the kitchen to get something to drink. When my father questioned where I had changed my clothes, I was taken aback that he had even noticed. I guess he knew that I didn't leave the house looking the same way I did when I came home. Quickly, I lied and told him I got caught in the rain and changed at Taylor's house. That was the benefit of being raised in a hustling household – it was second nature for me to lie on the spot.

"Did anybody call me?" I asked from the kitchen, trying to stay as far away from them as possible.

Even with all the washing up and wardrobe changing I had done at Taylor's house, I thought if they got a good look at me, they would know my dirty little secret.

"Nobody called. The secretary doesn't have any messages for you tonight boss," my mother teased.

My father, who always thought he was the comedian in the family, coached her along. "Good one, Deb."

They both laughed, slapping fives with each other at what they considered was a witty comeback. It was cute to me. Their bond wasn't something I saw too much of growing up in the hood.

"All right Frick and Frack, I'm going to bed." I still didn't want to spend too much time in their presence.

I kissed them both good night before making my way to my bedroom. But when I kissed my father, I felt a surge of guilt gnaw at my heart. I wasn't Daddy's little girl anymore. In that swift of an instance, I had become another man's woman.

Chapter 6

"**S**o, I saw you and Malik together the other day. What's up with y'all?" Reece asked.

We were sitting on the hill which had become the unofficial gathering spot for all the local teenagers. Whatever we felt we needed and everything we thought we wanted could be found in that one spot. Ironically, the Community Center was also on the hill. It offered free computer classes, art sessions and karate lessons every day of the week. However, we seemed to find much more exciting activities sitting outside. There was too much going on in the streets to be locked up in the Center listening to some old ass teacher talking about a damn computer program. We just knew we'd never need to know anything about computers in our adult lives.

"Nothing, we just chilling."

The first rule of the game was to keep my business to myself. Problems would undoubtedly arise as a result of too many people having their noses all up in it.

Malik and I had been seeing each other on the down low for about three months. I became a regular at apartment 6F. Bandit didn't bother barking at me anymore when I came into the crib. Taylor was right about not sweating him because before I knew it, he was all on my shit.

We were chilling, things were good and I was having fun.

We went for rides out to Far Rockaway all the time. Even the people out there knew my name. Malik took me shopping, got my nails done and always kept money in my pockets.

We were sexing like crazy and it even started feeling better. I was getting on top and letting him hit it from the back. I even went down on him a few times but the taste of cum in my mouth made me want to gag.

It was, and still is, an acquired taste.

I heard the sounds of bass coming from a car's speakers as it approached the hill. I crossed my fingers and hoped it was Malik. When the car got closer, I noticed it was. He stopped and summoned me over. I jumped up with the quickness and looked back at my friends as if they were inferior. They all thought he was stopping for one of them.

"Hey Malik." My smile beamed from one ear to the other.

"Get in the car," he barked without bothering to look at me while he spoke. "See if your friends wanna come with you."

I could tell by his face that something was wrong.

"What happened?"

"Yo," he yelled, "you coming or what?"

I turned to my friends who were already getting up off of the benches. It was like they had been listening the whole time and knew what I was going to say before I had a chance say it. We hopped in the car and of course I sat in the front – that occurred without a second thought.

"Malik, where we going?" Kia asked.

"Oh, we about to go out to Brooklyn. This kid just ran up on my brother and shit. I gotta go see what's up."

It was obvious that he was anxious about something, that much I could tell. Regardless, I was pissed that he told Kia what was wrong and didn't bother mentioning it to me. I made a mental note to bring that up with him later on when we were alone. I wasn't about to let my friends see me getting all upset over it.

We pulled up to his mother's two-family house on the corner of Monroe Street in the heart of Bed-Stuy. I had never met her before and to make matters worse, I was wearing a black t-shirt with bold white letters that read "Fuck The World".

What a way to make a first impression.

We climbed up the rickety steps leading to his mother's door when Malik turned around and passed me the biscuit.

"Hold this." He stuffed the gun down my shorts. "I can't go in there with this on me."

I pulled my shirt out hoping to cover it but it was no help. The handle still protruded from my waistband. But that time when he gave me my responsibility, I wasn't scared at all. I knew there were certain things a hustler's lady had to do. It wasn't the first time I held his gun either. Whenever we went out to Far Rockaway, I would hold it and be his protector just like Bonnie was to Clyde. So when he handed it to me, I took it and didn't think twice.

As we entered the living room, the first thing I noticed was an open Bible on the wooden coffee table. Old school Mahalia Jackson gospel music played on the portable radio that was propped up against some dusty books on the end table. There was the traditional velvet picture of the Black Jesus which hung on the wall directly adjacent to the couch. We sat there and looked at the picture as Black Jesus looked back at us.

I thought it was ironic that a devout church woman was also the mother of one of the biggest drug dealers in Queensbridge. Immediately, I remembered the shirt I was wearing.

"*Shit,*" I thought to myself. "*I need to turn my shirt inside out. I can't meet his mother wearing this!*"

"Where's the bathroom?" I asked Malik while he was in deep conversation with his brother.

He stopped in mid-sentence and gave me an aggravated look.

"Don't you see I'm talking? It's over there." He pointed toward the closed door on the other side of the house.

I jumped off the couch and stomped my way across the living room. I didn't know why the fuck he was so irritated with me. He knew how his mother was so he shouldn't have brought me there wearing that shirt. The least he could've done was warned me before we got out of the car. If anyone should have had an attitude, it should have been me.

Before I could get to the bathroom, his mother stepped out of the kitchen and stopped dead smack in front of me. Dumbfounded, I couldn't muster up any words to say. We had never been introduced and there I was strolling through her house.

"Hello, you must be Mrs. Brown. Hi, I'm um, I'm Chaka." I managed to spit out a few words despite the lump forming in my throat.

I reached my hand out in hopes that she'd shake it. She did and her grip was strong. She towered me so I had to look up to meet her eyes, which at that very point were reading my "Fuck The World" t-shirt. She hated me from the start.

Her height was intimidating. I figured she was about six feet tall and that was while she was wearing her house slippers. She wasn't overweight but her body was solid. Her skin was a lighter shade of brown than Malik's and she wore her jet black wavy hair tightly pulled back into a bun. She was beautiful but her eyes were hardened as though life for her had never been a crystal stair.

"Hello," she growled.

Barry White had nothing on that woman's deep baritone voice. If she did sing in her church choir, she was definitely an alto or maybe even a tenor.

"Um, nice to, um, meet you. I've heard so much about you."

I was trying to make polite small talk as I glanced at Malik, hoping he'd come over and interrupt us.

"Is that so?" She didn't try to sound any nicer. "Well I ain't never heard about you."

"Ma," Malik yelled across the living room.

Well, about fucking time.

"Malik, I done told you time and time again that this house ain't no hotel." Mrs. Brown spoke loudly while walking toward her son with her arms outstretched.

She embraced him and shook her head. "Boy, I pray for you every night. I swear before Jesus that I pray for you."

Just as their little impromptu Oedipus-type reunion was getting underway, someone yelled up to the window.

"Get your bitch ass down here."

It sounded as if there were a group of henchmen all outside waiting for Malik's brother.

"That's them?" He asked.

The fear on his brother's face was evident as he hesitantly nodded his head yes. Suddenly in the middle of the living room, right in front of his mother and my friends, Malik ran to me and pulled the gun out of my shorts. My eyes opened wide and my heart beat furiously. The sound of the gun cocking back to release a bullet into the chamber resonated throughout the house as Malik and his brother ran downstairs.

"LORD JESUS NO," Mrs. Brown screamed.

None of us knew what to do. My friends were stuck on the couch not knowing whether they should duck or get up and run. Everything was happening so quickly.

"You brought a gun in my house? Satan get thee out of my house." Mrs. Brown knelt in front of the Black Jesus picture as she continued to hoot and holler.

"Chaka call the police," Reece pleaded, just like a little bitch.

"No, I ain't calling no police. For what, so he could get arrested? Just chill, he got this."

I ran to the window despite Mrs. Brown's ranting, raving and speaking in tongues. From the crack in the mini-blinds, I could see Malik with his hand in his pocket firmly holding the gat. He was arguing with the kid and I could tell by his fearful expression that he knew Malik was packing heat. That nigga wasn't getting loud or nothing. Instead, he seemed to be copping a plea. Even his group of friends was just standing there all quiet and shit. Malik had the power in that situation.

I paid no attention to the fact that I had just disrespected his mother's house or that Malik could have blown that kid's head off at any moment. All I could think about was how proud I was that my man could pump the fear of God into somebody else.

Mrs. Brown stayed in the living room loudly reciting Bible scriptures. From the corner of my eye I could see her pacing back and forth, screaming at the top of her lungs. Spit flew out of her mouth spraying all over my friends who were still perched on the couch. I was glad I was standing by the window because I didn't need a sermon from the likes of Mommy fucking Dearest.

I turned my attention back to Malik as the group of dudes walked off in the face of defeat. As if he knew I'd be watching, he looked up to the window and motioned for me to come downstairs. His sinister grin made me giggle out loud. I grabbed his car keys from off of the table and told my friends it was time to leave.

"Mrs. Brown, I'm really sorry about all of this. It was really nice meeting you."

"Honey, I'ma be praying for you. Lord knows being around my son, you gonna need all the prayers you could get. Mark my words, that boy ain't nothing but trouble. You'll see. If God is my witness, you'll see."

Her words slightly haunted me as we made our way down the stairs and onto the corner.

"Get in the car y'all. Everything is all right now," Malik said.

He gave his brother a quick hug and hopped into the driver's seat. As soon as we pulled off, I let him have it. I didn't care who was in the car with us.

"Yo, why did you do that shit right in front of your mother?" I was yelling at the top of my lungs, demanding an explanation.

"Who the fuck you think you talking to like that Chaka?" Malik seemed surprised that I was flipping on him.

"I'm talking to you nigga."

"You better watch your mouth before you get hurt. I ain't in the mood for your bullshit and that's my word."

I felt Sheena poke me in the side from the back seat. I guess she wanted me to shut up. I was having none of that. I needed to get my point across.

"No, fuck that Sheena! Fuck him! How you gonna pull a gun out in front of your moms like that? You don't know how that shit made me look."

"I told you to shut the fuck up." Malik started yelling even louder than me.

"You told me to shut up? My own father don't tell me to shut up. Who the fuck are you? FUCK YOU!"

As soon as the last word rolled off my tongue, Malik immediately pulled the car over. He jumped out of his seat and stormed to the passenger side door.

"Get the fuck out the car."

He moved so swiftly that I didn't have time to lock the door before he flung it open.

I ignored him thinking he was about to come up with some sorry ass apology for making me look bad in front of his mother. I figured he would close the door and realize he had a lot of making up to do. My thoughts couldn't have been further from the truth.

My head jerked as he yanked a handful of my hair pulling me down to the ground. He scraped my body along the concrete sidewalk while I kept reaching up above my head trying to pry his hands off of me. The more I reached, the tighter he gripped.

He had never put his hands on me. In fact, no man had ever beaten on me like that.

"Who you think you talking to? I ain't no bitch ass nigga from off the streets."

Suddenly I felt his knuckles crack against the side of my cheek. For a moment, everything went black. Blood gushed from my mouth as I tried to scream.

"Somebody help me."

"Oh now you want somebody to help you. Where's all that mouth you had in the car you stupid bitch?"

Malik lifted his leg high off the ground and his Timberland boot came stomping against my stomach. My body automatically crawled into a fetal position to lessen the intensity of his blows but it didn't help at all. Groggily, I glanced over to the car and saw my friends watching everything with bated breath.

"The next time I tell you to shut up, you better shut the fuck up."

A punch or a kick accompanied his every word. I looked into his eyes and nothing was familiar. He had a dazed glare like he was possessed. My vision was blurred but I could make out the back of his hand as it got closer to my face. Before I could move out of its path, I heard a loud thump. My left eye began twitching as it connected with his blow. I felt it swelling to the point where I couldn't fully open it. I looked down and watched the blood as it spilled from my mouth and covered the white letters of my "Fuck The World" t-shirt.

"I'M SORRY, I'M SORRY, I'M SORRY."

I had no idea what I was sorry about. I just knew I wanted him to stop pounding on me. It had gotten so bad that I could no longer feel any pain.

"You see what you made me do," he panted.

Finally, he had beaten me so much that he was out of breath.

"Malik please, I'm sorry, I'm sorry."

My tears continued to fall down my bruised face.

He pulled me up from off of the ground and threw me back into the car. Remembering my friends were in the back seat, I tried to muffle the sounds of my cries. I wasn't going to give them the satisfaction of actually looking at my face so I didn't bother to turn around. All I wanted to do was to run to my mother's arms and beg her to console me. She was the only person that could make it all better.

"Are you good?" Sheena whispered into my ear from the back seat before Malik had a chance to get into the car.

I didn't respond. She just sat there and watched me get brutalized, not even two minutes before, and then had the nerve to ask me if I was good? To be honest, I didn't expect Reece and Kia to do anything to help me. They were probably amused throughout the whole ordeal. But Sheena was supposed to be my best friend. I felt betrayed by her and betrayed by Malik. Most of all, I felt betrayed by God. How could God have let that happen to me?

The ride back to Queensbridge was silent but full of tears. My heart hurt far more than my body. I kept telling myself that if Malik loved me, he would have never done that to me.

I'm still not sure if it was the beating that hurt more or the thought of him not loving me.

I hadn't realized we were off the highway until I heard my friends say goodbye as they all exited the car. I watched them disappear into the block and could have sworn I saw Reece and Kia start laughing once they thought I couldn't see them anymore.

"Malik, I can't go home like this." I could barely mumble the words out of my swollen mouth.

What was I supposed to do? What would my family say if they saw me like that? My seventeenth birthday was two days away and there I was looking like I had just finished sparring with Mike Tyson. There was no way that could have been a happy birthday. Instead of looking forward to it, I was wishing I was dead or that I had never been born at all.

He parked the car on a deserted street and touched the side of my face. Although I couldn't bear the sight of him, still my heart ached for him to love me back.

"Baby, I'm sorry. I didn't mean to hurt you like this."

As I heard his voice and felt his hands caressing my bruises, my body crumbled with uncontrollable sobs.

"How could you do this to me?"

The question was rhetorical. I really didn't expect him to answer. For the life of me I couldn't understand how the man I loved could turn so violent. That was the type of shit I watched on talk shows with those dumb ass housewives not something I expected to encounter at sixteen.

"Look at my face, Malik. Look at it."

Of course, I was too scared to pull the mirror down from the visor above my seat and look at it myself. Just by feeling the swelling and seeing the blood, I could pretty much picture what I must've looked like.

"Chak, I know you gonna leave me now. But just know that I love you and I didn't mean to hurt you," he whispered into my ear.

"You don't love me. How could you love me and hurt me like this?"

"I promise Baby, this won't ever happen again. I was just stressed out with this shit with my brother. I'm sorry, Chako, I love you."

Tears began to form in his eyes as he spoke. I thought he had to be telling me the truth because niggas just didn't cry for no reason. I knew he was stressed and I only pushed him to flip out the way he did. I blamed myself for his actions. It had to have been my fault.

"I love you too," I cried.

Malik held me in his arms and gently wiped my tears.

"You know you have to stay at the crib for a little while until your face heals up."

What else was there for me to do at that point? I couldn't go home and explain to my mother that I was assaulted by my grown ass boyfriend whom she knew nothing about. She wouldn't understand that people made mistakes sometimes. She'd want to call the police and get all extra about the situation. So, I did the only thing I thought I could do. I agreed to stay with him.

We went up to apartment 6F the usual way. He walked in the building first and I waited five minutes before I entered. I held my head down so nobody would be able to see my face.

When I got there, he let me into the apartment and explained to me that he had to go home. I understood. He wasn't my man. He gave me a kiss on the cheek and again apologized for everything. Before I had a chance to respond, he was already heading out the door. As it closed and the lock turned, I finally realized that I was all by myself. Alone, except for the comfort of a crazed Rottweiler named Bandit.

I cried myself to sleep on the small rusty-framed twin size mattress. That night wouldn't be the last time I cried alone.

Chapter 7

"**H**appy Birthday"
The sound of Malik's voice jolted me out of my sleep.
My left eye was still swollen shut.

Although I hadn't looked at myself in the mirror, I could
tell from the pain that I was in bad shape. With my right eye,
I saw him sitting at the foot of the bed. He had flowers in one
hand and two gift-wrapped boxes in the other, one big and
one small. That was the first time I had seen him since the day
he attacked me.

"Hey Chako," he whispered. "Happy Birthday Baby."

Obviously he had no problem with the lumps formed
around my face because he kissed me right in my plumped
lips.

"Thank you. Is that for me?" I pointed to the boxes.

"No it's for some other pretty girl with a birthday today."

He handed them to me, along with a beautiful bouquet of
red long stem roses. Until he arrived, I hadn't realized I had
been in the apartment for two days.

"They're beautiful." I tried to smile despite how painful it
was to move my mouth.

I sat up in bed and began to open the boxes. Truly, I wanted
to be happy but inside I couldn't stop thinking about my
mother and how I wanted to be with her instead. I pulled the

pink DKNY vest and matching jean shorts from out of the first box. Underneath the outfit was a red lace bra and panty set from Victoria's Secret. Malik must not have paid any attention to my breasts because he bought a size 36D and I was barely fitting into an A-cup.

The smaller box had to be jewelry. It wasn't big enough to fit anything else. Before everything went bad, I had asked him for a pair of earrings so I knew what the gift would be. I opened the box to find two big gold hoops. They looked just like the ones he ripped out of my ears two days before.

I managed to utter a half ass thank you before breaking down in tears. I wished I could have spent that day with my family. That was the day my mother gave birth to me yet at that moment, she didn't know if I was dead or alive. I wanted to call her but I wouldn't know what to say. When I closed my eyes, I could picture her sitting on the couch crying. Every time the phone rang, I knew she thought it was me. But, I couldn't go home, not yet anyway.

Without asking what was wrong, Malik started kissing on my neck. He pulled up my t-shirt and pushed my panties to the side as I leaned back onto the bed. Instead of undressing, he pulled his penis out of the zipper opening of his pants and thrust it into me. Routinely, I spread my legs apart to let him inside. Sex seldom lasted long. Just long enough for him to cum. After about ten minutes of pumping, he fulfilled his mission and was getting dressed to go back out again.

"Are you leaving?" I was desperate for some company. After all, it was my birthday and I didn't want to be alone.

"Yeah, I was supposed to meet Jamere fifteen minutes ago," Malik quickly answered while I followed him, like a lap dog, into the living room.

There was a knock on the door and before I had a chance to run back into the bedroom, he opened it. The expression on Jamere's face was evident as soon as he walked into the apartment. He looked at me with pity and at Malik with disgust. On the other hand, Malik showed no signs of shame whatsoever. He just didn't give a fuck about it one way or the other.

Jamere didn't say a word. He didn't have to because I

already knew what he was thinking. He warned me about Malik and I should've taken heed.

"Hey you, cat got your tongue?" I had to say something to break the awkwardness in the air.

"Nah baby girl, how you doing?"

I could tell from his response that he didn't know what else to say. The longer he stood there, the more he tried to avert his attention away from my face.

"I'm all right. Can't you tell?"

Malik shot me a glance that quietly told me not to say another word and that time I knew better. He said he would never hit me again, and although I believed him, I didn't want to take any chances.

"So, when are you getting on the road?" Malik turned back toward Jamere as he spoke.

"As soon as possible. I'm just waiting for this cat to come through with my money and then I'm out."

"On the road to where?" Surely I was taking a risk by talking to Jamere but if he was leaving I had to know where he was going.

"Oh, I'm moving down to Atlanta."

"Atlanta? You got family out there or something?" I was confused as to why anyone would want to leave Queensbridge, let alone New York.

"Nah, just business. The hood is over for me. It's time to step out and do some other stuff. I'm getting too old for this nickel and dime, you know what I mean, Chak. You should think about moving down south. There's a lot of cats from New York down there."

Malik was quick to interject with his disapproval of that notion. "Nah, Chaka ain't leaving me. She love it right here. Her down south, yeah right, that shit is too slow. Right, Ma?"

"Yeah, I guess so." I looked at Malik and faked a smile.

I was kind of heartbroken that Jamere was really leaving. So, without even bothering to say goodbye, I turned and walked into the bedroom. My eyes were filling with tears and the last thing I needed was for either of them to see me cry. The door slammed loudly as they left the apartment.

"Dag," I whispered to myself, "he could've at least said bye."

Since sleep was the only thing I could do, I lied down and drifted off.

KNOCK - KNOCK - KNOCK

It sounded as if the police were about to kick the door down and raid the spot. Since Malik had a key, I knew he wasn't out there knocking like a maniac.

KNOCK - KNOCK - KNOCK

And if it was the police, the last thing they'd be doing was knocking. Those bastards would have just kicked the door off the hinges. I sat up on the bed and thought for a minute. The only other person who knew I was there was Jamere. With that hope, I quickly headed toward the front door.

As I walked by the dining room table, I noticed Malik had taken Bandit with him and left me a fifty dollar bill lying in plain view. The money was his way of saying he had no intentions on returning.

I looked through the peephole expecting to see Jamere. Instead, it was Zakia and Ta-Ta, the girls from that other clique.

Shit, I cursed myself for getting up. They had to have seen me look through the peephole so I couldn't act like I wasn't there.

KNOCK – KNOCK – KNOCK

"Just a minute," I yelled.

Frantically, I buzzed around the apartment searching for anything I could use to hide my face. As I rummaged through the junk drawers in the kitchen, I found an old pair of sunglasses. They were buried under a bunch of unopened envelopes, dingy rubber bands, rusty nail clippers, sticky packs of duck sauce and a host of other unnecessary bullshit. The frames were coated with about an inch of dust. They were nearly two sizes too big for my slender face but they were dark enough to cover my eyes so they were better than nothing. I pulled a butter knife out of the drawer and checked out my reflection for the first time since being in that apartment.

Damn, I was still a mess.

After taking a long deep breath, I opened the door and let them in. Curiosity got the best of me and thoughts scattered through my mind as to why they were there. I mean, they were my friends and all that but they weren't my clique.

"Hey girl, how you doing?" Zakia gave me a brief but unexpected hug.

She was only two or three years older than me but she acted like Mother Hen. Her long flowy hair was always hooked up in a banging doobie which the Dominicans kept fresh every week. Her beauty wasn't typical but she had sort of an exotic look about her. Even her nails were eccentric as they were so long they curved. She emphasized their length with every intricate airbrushed design available in the Vietnamese nail shop. With her full lips and large forehead, she could have passed for Sade, except she was chestnut brown with a cracked front tooth that was turning black.

They sat on the old battered couch and I stood near the broken metal chairs. There was less light where I was standing so I thought they wouldn't be able to really get a good look at my face. We engaged in small talk for a while but I could tell they were trying to pretend not to see my bruises.

"Yo, fuck all this bullshit y'all talking about right now," Ta-Ta blurted out as she jumped up off the couch. "What the fuck happened to your face?"

Even at such a young age, she always kept it real.

Ta-Ta was Zakia's little sister. The bitch was only fifteen but she carried herself like she was thirty. Hustling was in her nature. She knew the streets like the back of her hand. Everybody said she was too grown for her own good but that was because she could easily intimidate people of all ages. Being short was about the only thing Ta-Ta and Zakia had in common. Ta-Ta's skin was smooth and creamy like dark chocolate. Her big titties were disproportional to her flat white-girl ass and tiny waist. Her breasts were firm, voluptuous and perkily sat up even without a bra. Fuchsia highlights poked through her jet black bob cut. She wouldn't be caught in the streets without the latest fashions – Prada, Gucci, Louis Vuitton. Although she claimed they were real, she had really bought her labels from the Chinese immigrants down on Fulton Street in Brooklyn. Ta-Ta had it going on for a young buck. What Zakia lacked in bluntness, her little sister sure made up for it.

"You think those droopy ass sunglasses is hiding anything? Puhleeze! Matter of fact, take these shits off." Ta-Ta grabbed the glasses off of my face and tossed them on the other side of the room. "That's what the fuck we talking about right fucking there."

She pointed to my eyes as she got closer and her screams grew louder and more animated. The way she was yelling, you would think it was her face that was all fucked up.

"Why does it matter to you what happened to my face?" I had to force my voice, which was semi-horse from crying so much, to be louder than hers.

"Because we're your friends, Chaka." Zakia stood firmly in between Ta-Ta and I while holding her hands on both of our chests to back us up from one another.

"Y'all ain't my friends. Y'all just wanna be nosy. Fuck y'all."

It was me against the world. My only friend was Malik. I moved back from Zakia and sat down on the metal chair to regain my composure. The last thing I needed was another fight.

Ta-Ta, who was offended by my remark, raised her voice ten octaves higher and started smacking her hands together on every syllable in an attempt to emphasize her point.

"Oh, if we ain't your friends then who the fuck is your friends? It damn sure ain't Reece and Kia. They running around telling everybody that Malik stomped you out. But those is your friends, right?"

I looked at Zakia for confirmation on whether or not she was telling the truth.

"Yeah." She nodded her head in agreement. "How do you

think we knew you were here?"

"So everybody knows what happened?"

What I thought was my secret was floating around the projects like a hot off the press news release. And my friends, my clique, were the people reporting it.

"Yeah and they even told everybody you ain't been home and your Moms is looking all over for you. Hmmm, but those is your friends right?" Ta-Ta took a seat and crossed her legs, satisfied she had gotten her point across.

Her words rang true as she folded her arms and leaned back in her chair. Those bitches were not my friends at all, not even Sheena.

"That's enough, Ta-Ta." Zakia tried her hardest to speak calmly once she turned back toward where I was sitting.

"Chaka we didn't come over here to argue with you. We just wanted to know how you were doing, that's all. You know, make sure you all right."

She stood next to the broken metal folding chair and rubbed my back. Ta-Ta continued looking at me but stayed mute, which had to have been a first for her.

"I mean, damn, look at your face. You're too pretty for this," Zakia continued. "If he loved you he wouldn't do this to you."

"Look, I appreciate y'all coming over but me and Malik got this. For real, he ain't never gonna hit me no more."

I felt the more I said it, the more I would believe it.

They got up to leave and once again I was hit with a pang of loneliness. I knew Malik wouldn't be back any time soon. He left me fifty dollars but he didn't leave a key so there was no way I could go out and spend it.

"Are y'all in a rush?" I jumped up and stopped them before they could open the door.

"No, not really. Do you want us to stay?" Zakia could sense the pleading in my voice.

"Yeah, if y'all want."

"Well, only if you got something to drink up in this crackhead-ass, piece of shit crib," Ta-Ta joked.

I pulled a six-pack of Heinekens from the refrigerator just

as she held up an already rolled blunt in one hand and a pink Bic lighter in the other.

"Well shit, we ain't going nowhere then," she said.

We all laughed as Ta-Ta sparked the bud and began the cypher. It was the first time I had laughed in two days. We talked for hours about shit I didn't even know we had in common. We were all in sync. I felt like I had been a part of their clique for years.

"Oh, and by the way, today is my birthday." I finally admitted.

"Well Happy fuckin' Birthday!"

Zakia and Ta-Ta both started singing Stevie Wonder's black version of the ever popular birthday song.

We embraced, and for a second, I was happy. I didn't think about Malik. I didn't think about my mother. All I thought about were my new friends. That was the beginning of a long friendship and regardless of whatever went down, at that moment I knew, we would be friends for life.

CHAPTER 8

More than a week had gone by and my face seemed to be healing. The longer I stayed there, the harder it would be for me to leave. I was nervous and didn't know what to expect when I got home. Whatever happened, I just had to deal with it. It had finally hit me, that within the span of a few days, my whole existence had changed.

I waited until it was dark outside before heading back to my mother's house. Malik was barely around during the whole time that I stayed there. In fact, he only showed up once in a blue moon, so I doubted if he'd even realize whether or not I had gone home. I was glad he finally left me a key even though I was still too embarrassed to venture out.

I made it through the block without being noticed, which was hard in a place where everybody was trying to know what the fuck was going on with everybody else. As I entered my building, I thought about going to Taylor's crib first to get a feel for how shit was going down at my house. I thought if I could persuade Taylor into coming home with me then maybe my mother wouldn't flip out so badly. But I was fooling myself because she wouldn't have given a damn about my cousin being there or not. Whatever awaited me was something I had to face on my own.

I took a deep breath before sliding my key into the lock.

Despite my twists and turns of the key, the door wouldn't open. I took it out and examined it more closely to make sure it was the right one. Since it was, I tried it again but it still didn't work.

"Damn," I thought, *"something must be wrong with this stupid ass lock. Everything around this motherfucker is always broken."*

Fed up with the key not working, I knocked on the door and hoped for somebody to be home. Before I could take my hand off the knocker, my mother opened it. She looked so different. I could tell by the swelling of her eyes that she had been crying. Her hair, which she usually kept neatly pressed and curled, was loosely pulled back into a ponytail. Gray strands poked out from around her edges. Prior to that day, I had never noticed that she had gray hair.

My mother didn't give me a chance to walk through the door before she wrapped her arms around me and hugged me real tight. She started crying which made me burst into tears.

"My baby, you're all right."

With every word, she looked at me and touched my face. She didn't ask any questions but I could tell by the way she looked at me, that she knew.

We finally made it into the apartment where my mother held me even tighter. Walking through the dining room, the first thing I noticed was two suitcases tucked under the table. I thought it was peculiar for them to be planning a trip without me.

What if I hadn't come home, would they have still left anyway?

My picture was the second thing I noticed on top of the black lacquer entertainment center. It was underneath a glassed white candle like the Spanish people buy from the corner bodega. It had a drawing of the Virgin Mary on the front and a prayer inscribed on the casing in the back. It was some true Santeria shit.

My house felt strange. It wasn't full of laughter and happiness as it had always been. The lights were dim and although the television was on, there was no sound coming out of it. When I looked at the screen, I instantly recognized images of me in my sixth grade play. I was dressed up like an elf. It must have been Christmas time or something.

"Where have you been? I've been so worried." My mother sat less than an inch away from me on the couch. She wouldn't let go of my hand as tears poured out of her eyes.

"Mommy, I'm sorry. Please don't be mad."

I wanted to tell her everything that happened from the beginning to the end. But I couldn't. There was no way she'd understand how my life had changed so abruptly. Pulling my hair away from my face, she held my chin slowly and turned my head from side to side. Though I had healed up a little, I knew I couldn't pass her inspection.

"What happened? Who did this to you?"

She was begging for an answer that I just couldn't give her. And God knows she deserved some sort of explanation but I couldn't fix my mouth to say anything.

"Mommy, I'm sorry."

My body collapsed in her arms. She held me close and let me cry. I was telling her everything without ever verbalizing anything. And she listened. Every tear told the story behind my absence. I felt like her baby again. My mother would protect me. As I cried in her arms, all the pain poured from my heart and into hers.

"It's all right. Don't talk now, baby, I'm here."

My mother cried with me as if she fully understood the pain I had endured over the past few days. Gently, she ran her fingers through my hair. All my worries disappeared as she seemed to take all my pain away as only a mother could. Through my tears, she let me give it all to her.

"What is she doing here?"

Looking up, I realized it was my father speaking. He was an average sized man and slim in stature, but at that moment, he looked like a giant. All of a sudden, I was scared again.

"Daddy, I'm sorry. I..."

He interrupted before I could finish my sentence.

"I don't want to hear all that bullshit. Your bags are over there." He pointed toward the suitcases under the dining room table. "You wanna run the streets? Then go 'head."

My father calmly walked over to the bags, picked them up and placed them at my feet. I looked at him, looked at the suitcases and looked back up at him again somewhat perplexed. Then it finally hit me. I was the only one leaving the house that night. My keys weren't messed up, they had changed the locks. They were kicking me out.

"Mommy," I yelled, "what is he talking about?"

I knew talking to my father wouldn't have changed a thing. The crocodile tears never worked on Daddy anyway. But wasn't I his little girl? How could he do that to me?

"Fred, no, she doesn't have anywhere to go," my mother said.

"Well she had somewhere to go for the past two weeks. Let her grown ass go back there."

"It's ok, we talked about it. She's not gonna do that again." My mother was pleading her case through her hysterics but it didn't seem to be working.

She ran to Daddy's side, grabbed his arms and looked directly into his eyes as she spoke. As for me, I immediately reverted to what I knew best and I jumped to my defense.

"You want me to leave? Fine, I'll leave. I don't wanna be here anyway."

From a distance, I could hear the neighbors' doors opening up as they poked out to see what was going on.

"No Chaka, just sit down. Let me handle this. You don't have to leave." My mother ran to my side attempting to stop me from walking out of the door. "Let's just talk about this please."

"Ain't no talking about nothing no more. She wants to be grown, let her ass be grown. She won't last a month out there on those streets," my father yelled.

"Oh, I won't? Yeah, we'll see. I'm grown. I don't need you. I don't need anybody. I can make it on my own."

My tears were mixed with sadness and anger. I couldn't believe Daddy thought I was unable to survive without them. I'd show him just how wrong he was.

"Chaka, what are you doing? Don't say that. You can't make it out there yet. You don't even want to have to make it out there," my mother warned. "Trust me baby, please. Those streets ain't where you wanna be. Please trust me, just stop it."

My mother, who was usually soft-spoken, was trying to drown out my yelling by screaming even louder. Frantically, she ran to me and then ran to Daddy. It was like we were playing ping-pong with her heart and neither would give up until somebody lost.

"Oh, and you just gonna let him kick me out right?" I turned my anger toward her. "Fine, I don't need you either."

I picked up my bags and headed toward the door.

"CHAKA, NO." My mother grabbed me by the back of my new DKNY vest. "Freddy don't let her leave. She don't mean the things she's saying, please, no."

"Deb, let her go. She wasn't thinking about you while she was out there laying up." His response was emotionless and detached.

How did he know what I was thinking about?

Of course I thought about her. I cried myself to sleep thinking about the hell I was putting her through. The last person I wanted to hurt was my mother. She never deserved the way I treated her.

Ironically, that was a regret I would take with me for the rest of my life.

I sat my bags by my side and firmly walked over to Daddy. "What do you care? You ain't my REAL father anyway."

Before I had a chance to stop the words from coming out of my mouth, it was already too late. Everything just stopped. My mother stopped crying. Daddy stopped yelling. Nobody could believe what I had just said. I could tell Daddy was hurt. Although not biological, he was the only father I had ever known. I knew there was no going back from that point. The damage had been done. I had already said too much. It seemed like an eternity before either one of us reacted to my comment. But, I should have known what was coming next.

SMACK

I felt Daddy's rough hands scrape across my face. Limply I fell onto the floor. I had known better than to hit Daddy back. After being one man's punching bag, I didn't need any repeats of that.

Shrugging my mother's hands away from me, as she plunged to my side, I stood up and looked Daddy square in his face. Gone were the tears and the little girly feelings. I took a deep breath before speaking. I wanted my words to come out clear and concise.

"I hate you and I will never come back here. I don't need either one of y'all. I'll prove you both wrong and I'm gonna make it. I won't fail."

Daddy sensed that I meant exactly what I said. His look was as stern and stubborn as mine. We stood there staring into each other's eyes. My mother sat on the couch in tears, unable to fully understand what was going on. But Daddy knew. His eyes told me that he comprehended the situation perfectly. For the first time, he looked at me as a woman. His visions of his little girl and his need to protect me were gone. In its place was his understanding that he had to let me go. I had to move on. He couldn't guide me anymore. I needed to find my own way.

I stood straight up and held my head high as I grabbed both suitcases and walked toward the door. Gently placing a bag on the floor, I looked back one last time to catch a glimpse of my mother before I turned the door knob.

"No Freddy, don't let her leave."

She tried to get up and run to me but Daddy held her back. He knew the time had come for them to let me go.

"Chaka, NO," my mother cried. "Chaka, come back here."

I stood on the other side of the door as it slammed behind me, closing yet another chapter in my life. I wasn't a little girl anymore. Most importantly, I would never be their little girl ever again. When the reality of what happened finally hit me, the tears withheld from Daddy's sight, streamed down my face all at once.

Though I tried to block the sound, I could still hear my

mother yelling and crying from inside of the apartment. I placed one hand on the door wishing I could touch her heart instead. I said a silent prayer that God would bring her peace greater than the pain I had forced her to bear.

As I turned around, picked up my bags and walked down the stairs, I vowed to never look back. And under no circumstances, would I ever return.

Chapter 9

As I walked through my block and back to Malik's apartment, I grasped the fact that the only thing I had left was whatever Daddy packed into the two big ass suitcases I was lugging around. I didn't know what was in them but regardless of what it was, it was all I had to my name.

Looking up at Malik's window, I noticed the light was on in the living room which meant he was there. I clumsily journeyed on, stopping every few steps to sit my bags on the ground. Sweat ran profusely from my forehead. After all, I weighed about a hundred pounds and some change so the bags nearly outweighed me.

I wondered if Erika was up there with him. But then again, she was his lady and I knew he'd never bring her to a spot like that. As soon as I knocked on the door, Bandit started barking. The peephole opened and I saw Malik look through it.

"Hold on, let me put the muzzle on him," he said through the closed door.

After about a minute he opened up with a confused expression on his face. "What happened?"

"Well, you ain't gonna ask me to come in?" I snapped.

"Oh yeah, come in." He grabbed my suitcases and locked both locks on the door behind me as I entered.

"So Chak, what happened?"

"What do you think? They kicked me out, that's what's happened"

I figured it shouldn't have taken a rocket scientist to figure out why I was standing there with two suitcases.

"Word, what you gonna do?"

"What I'ma do?"

An awkward silence ensued which scared me for a moment because staying with him was my only option.

"Don't worry young love, we'll work this out. You'll be right here with me and Bandit," he chuckled as we sat down on the metal chairs seated at the folding table.

Truthfully speaking, I was glad to finally be out of my parents' house. No more curfew or people telling me what to do. And fuck school. I didn't feel like I was learning anything that I didn't already know any fucking way so I had no intentions on returning. I could stay with Malik all night if I wanted, just like a real grown-ass couple. Of course, I would have to do something about that apartment but other than that, I would be all right. I could sleep all day and fuck all night. I wouldn't have to go outside to sneak my weed or get drunk. Everything could be done from the comfort of my bed right next to my man. My father didn't realize it then but he actually did me a favor by kicking me out.

"What are you doing?" I asked.

There was a bright light in the lamp that hung above the table. Malik was sitting in front of a large glass plate and a scale. As I looked to his left, I noticed a shifter, some little baggies, a baby spoon and an ink pad with a stamp – like the stamps you get in the second grade when you do well on a test or something. On top of the plate was a huge mound of white powder that looked like a mini-version of Mt Everest. I knew perfectly well what Malik did for a living but up until that point, I hadn't seen it up close and personal.

"I'm bagging up some work right now. Come on and help me."

It must have been sweltering hot under that light because Malik was sweating so much that his nose was running.

"Well, what do I do?" I jumped to action, moving my chair closer to the table.

"First, let me get you some gloves."

Malik quickly passed me a pair of the hospital-type latex ones that he pulled from the junk drawer in the kitchen.

"Why do I need these?"

"You gotta put them on so the dope won't get all in your pores," he said.

I took the gloves and placed each one on my hands. They were a tight snug fit so I knew nothing was getting in there. He then passed me a surgical mask that covered my nose and mouth. I looked at it and was confused as to why it was needed but I promptly obliged. I glanced at Malik and noticed he was wearing neither the gloves nor the mask.

"How come you don't have this stuff on too?"

"I been doing this here thing for years. I don't need no gloves. I'm immune to this shit."

"All right," I shrugged. "Whatever. Well now what?"

I was ready to get to work. It was kind of romantic to be sitting in my new place working side by side with my man.

"First thing, take this measuring spoonful like this," Malik instructed with the spoon in his hand. "Take the powder, put it in the bag and then measure it on the scale. Make sure it's the right amount. We ain't giving these fiends nothing for free. If it's right, then seal the baggie and put this stamp on it."

I snickered when I realized we would be using a little kid's stamp on a bag of heroin.

"Well, why do we do that?"

I probably sounded like a five-year-old school girl asking all of those questions. But that drug game was some new shit to me.

"Well, you see the stamps have a dragon on them, right?" He held one of the bags up to the light to show me. "The name of my dope is White Dragon. When these fiends see the stamp, they know they getting the official White Dragon shit."

"Oh, the official shit, huh?" I laughed.

"No doubt."

He seemed to be in an unusually good mood all night. He was laughing and cracking jokes at my inexperience, continuously wiping sweat from his forehead and rubbing his nose. I assumed he was coming down with the flu or something so I didn't mention it. He was happy – real happy.

The seconds grew to minutes and the minutes to hours. I looked up at the clock and it was already two in the morning by the time we were done. Malik was still wide awake. It was my first night in my new apartment and I didn't want to be alone. I knew just what would knock his ass out and make him stay.

I stood up out of the wobbly chair and walked over to where Malik was sitting. Without saying a word, I knelt down on my knees, opened his pants and went to work. He grabbed my hair and guided my head up and down his hardening penis. I took it all in my mouth from the head all the way down to his balls. I deep throated him like my life depended on it. Shit, I had to give him a reason not to go home to Erika ever again. He moved my head harder and faster forcing his dick down my throat so far it nearly touched my esophagus. I was gasping for air but that didn't stop me. His moans let me know he was about to cum and when he did, I didn't move. I stayed right there with my mouth glued to the shaft of his dick.

Breathing hard, Malik lifted my face up to look at him and asked, "You really do love me don't you?"

With my jaws aching, I swallowed every drop of his cum before I responded. "And you better believe it."

"Come on baby, let's go to bed."

Malik picked me up from off of the floor and carried me to the bedroom as if we were newlyweds crossing the threshold.

That night we lay in each other's arms on our dingy twin size mattress until we fell asleep. I enjoyed my new independence and Malik enjoyed my company. After that night, he never went back to Erika. With me, he was home.

CHAPTER 10

"**N**ah girl, I ain't coming out. My furniture is supposed to be coming today. I gotta wait for the man to deliver it." I yelled into the speakerphone base while vacuuming the living room floor one last time before my couches arrived.

"Well, I'ma come over there and help you put everything together. You know how my technique is with lacing a crib. I'm on my way," Ta-Ta replied before hanging up.

As I looked around my apartment, I realized just how much things had changed over the past few months. Thanks to the money Malik was dishing out, I did a good job sprucing things up. If I had to live there, it had to be tight.

The first thing I did was got the walls painted. Usually, Housing would change the colors up every couple of years but since me nor Malik's name was on the lease, we couldn't make a request for them to do it. Instead, I paid a handy crackhead to paint them cream so they would match the wall-to-wall carpet I got installed. There was a plastic runner on the rug which led from the front door all the way to the bedroom. I wasn't about to let anybody ruin my carpet with their dirty shoes.

The living room window had beige vertical blinds which would perfectly complement the brown leather sofa and loveseat I was getting delivered. I lucked up and found some butter soft shit from Jennifer Convertibles Furniture on Queens Boulevard. Malik almost flipped when he found out how much it was all costing him but he knew I was a good girl to have on his team so I deserved only the best. Our 64-inch floor model television was placed, catty-cornered, in the living room near the window. On top of the TV was a silver DVD player and cable box that we got illegally zapped so we could get all the channels for free.

My end tables were part of a set that matched the glass coffee table. Shit, even the kitchen table was glass, and finally, all the chairs matched. However, I kept a folding card table in the closet for me and Malik to bag up the drugs. I wasn't about to shit at the same place where I had to eat.

Since the living room and dining room were so close together, I put up a wooden divider between the two in order to section them off into their own separate rooms.

The kitchen and bathroom were coordinated to a tee. I laid my own white and black ceramic tiles on the floor of both rooms and placed black blinds in the windows. My towels were black and white checkered as were the oven mitts which hung up from nails above the stove. The refrigerator was full of cutesy little magnets all over the door and always packed with food and Moët champagne. All the little extras like the microwave, the condiment containers and the plates – were red to give it a splash of color. My shit was looking like some shit I saw on television.

Malik finally threw away all those boxes piled up in the bedroom. Because the room seemed like it was about the size of a mini-van, we could only fit a Queen Size bed in there. I wanted a California King, but had I gotten one, there wouldn't have been room for anything else. And yes, I had to get the complete bedroom suite. The head and foot board had mirrors on it which was good for when Malik and I felt like getting a little freaky. The dresser was black marble as were the nightstands. I wanted the armoire but if I had gotten it, I would have had to put that shit in the damn bathroom just so I would have enough space to walk around the bed. The comforter, sheets and window blinds were gray to match my new swanky carpet.

I'm not sure how I did it but somehow I convinced Malik to finally get rid of that fleabag dog. I didn't know what he did with Bandit and I really didn't care. He was gone and I was happy about that.

The apartment was everything I had imagined it would be. It made me feel like a celebrity living in Hollywood, well in my case, Hollyhood.

Ta-Ta and I hung out on a daily basis. Since the day she and Zakia came to see me, we were inseparable. I saw Reece and the other bitches outside all the time. After all, the projects only consisted of six blocks so there was no way I wouldn't bump into them. I didn't speak to near one of them though. With a conceited twitch in my walk and my nose all up in the air, I strutted right on by their broke asses. Because Malik was with me, he didn't need them to ride around with him anymore. So they were always stuck, sitting on the hill and hoping to find another Captain Save-a-Hoe. Since they had already violated me by putting my business out there, I didn't give a fuck what they were doing.

Actually, I should have thanked them for running their mouths. Because of them, everybody in the hood knew that I was Malik's lady – his property. That title felt just like I thought it would. People who never spoke to me a day in their lives were going out of their way to say hello. Niggas who used to try to kick it to me knew they had to chill or they would deal with Malik, and trust me, they didn't want to do that. I walked through Queensbridge like royalty. I had notoriety. Finally, I felt like a somebody.

When I sat outside on the bench with my friends, we didn't have to exert any energy by walking to the store ourselves. Little kids ran up to me begging to go because they knew I would let them keep the change on a fifty dollar bill, even if we only bought some Chinese food for thirty.

All the little girls looked up to me. On Saturdays, I would take a selected few to the nail shop for manicures and pedicures. If they were really cute, I'd get them an outfit or a pair of sneakers. After all, their mothers were probably broke and sitting at home with too many damn kids to worry about anyway. Somebody had to show them the life they could live if they carried themselves the right way. To them, I was their American Idol.

Yet despite all the fake chicks that tried to befriend me, I only stuck with my crew – Zakia, Ta-Ta, Carmen, Sophie and Dana. We were the *"Sexy Six"* as niggas used to call us. Everybody in the clique had their own little thing about them and when we were together everything meshed.

Carmen was a beauty queen straight up. She was Cuban and Black so she had that good hair – long, thick and naturally curly. We nicknamed her Kelly Bundy because she acted like a dumb blonde half the time. Her long eyelashes had a natural curl which made her look like she was wearing mascara even though she never did. Her older brother was down with the Enforcers so she was well taken care of in the hood.

To hear Carmen speak was like listening to Rosie Perez in Spike Lee's, *Do the Right Thing.* Her accent was definitely exaggerated because her ass couldn't speak a lick of Spanish. But the dudes thought the way she talked was sexy so she used that to her advantage. Carmen could have easily been confused with one of those Puerto Rican mamis from Spanish Harlem. She dressed just like them with Levi jeans that were two sizes too tight which made her ass look sucked in like it had been hit with a bag of bricks. She always had on either a fresh pair of tan suede Timberlands or a pair of Fifty-Four-Elevens in mad different colors. She must have gotten her sense of color coordination from the Black side of her family because Cubans never matched.

Carmen was lucky. She was one of those high yellow model looking type of girls. Her brother, Carlos, always made sure she had money and fly clothes. The only thing she needed from a nigga was some dick, and true to hot Latina form, she got plenty of it.

Dana was the crazy and wildest one of us all. She stood almost six feet tall and was borderline anorexic-looking. She could have been in the WNBA but she was too much into the streets for all that. Her complexion was mahogany brown with perfectly shaped white teeth. She made it her business to smile hard enough to show them off every chance she got. Her eyes were squinty like she was Chinese or something. It was easy to tell when we got blunted just by looking at Dana's eyes.

Stylishly subtle and more laid back than the typical project bitch, she was the only one out of our clique who wore linen suits and slacks. Although she had the shape for them, she never wore hottie clothes. According to Dana, she wanted to maintain her classy. Come to think of it, she's the one that put me up on designers like Armani, Ann Taylor and Tahari. Before that, I only knew about Gucci and Louis Vuitton. You know, the hood shit with the logos.

However, it was hard to maintain her classy when she was pissy drunk, which was the way Dana liked to be. She was the type of chick who would get bent and start singing old love songs with a drink in her hand. And, she knew all the old school jams too, like Gerald Levert and Christopher Williams. The words would be fucked up but usually we were all a little too drunk to even notice.

Sophie was the odd ball out of the crew. She was the Afrocentric positive chick with morals and other unnecessary bullshit. I don't know what she had in common with us because she was on a whole different level. She graduated from high school and was taking classes at La'Guardia Community College. Sophie kept a job and never fucked with any of the project niggas. She was short and light skinned with barely visible freckles on her face. Her hair was naturally red and she kept it in long kinky twists all the time. She wore thin gold framed glasses which gave her an even more educated look.

"Get a job, go to school and don't depend on a man for anything." Sophie was always trying to school us.

She was closer to Zakia's age and had a daughter. So, those two were sort of their own mini-clique most of the time. She wasn't completely annoying but I had to explain to her on more than one occasion that I didn't need a job because Malik would always make sure I was living right.

The phone rang a few times before I picked it up. I had a rule, answering on the first one made you look anxious for a call. So no matter what, I always let it ring at least three times.

"Hello."

"Hey Chaka, what you doing?"

I had hoped it was the furniture delivery man but when I

heard her voice, I knew it was Taylor.

"Nothing, just waiting on my furniture."

"Girl, I gotta tell you something but you gotta promise not to get mad," she said.

How could she have expected me not to get mad when I had no idea what she was going to say? Usually when people precede a comment like that, it means the next thing to come out of their mouths will piss you the fuck off anyway.

"Taylor, I promise. Now come on, what is it?" I was growing anxious to hear the gossip.

"Girl, I was talking to Keisha last night and she told me she was at Jackson Hole Diner. You know the one right next to the Airway Motel, right?" She paused to make sure I knew the location.

"Yeah, I know. Oooooh, she's so nasty. Who had Keisha's ugly ass up in the Airway?"

"Never mind all that. Anyway, she was there and in walked Malik and Reece."

"WHAT?" I almost dropped the phone once I heard the names. "They were together?"

"Chaka, would I be telling you about it if they weren't together? But yeah, so, Keisha told me because she knows we're family. She said the way they were all up on top of each other, that it wasn't just food bringing them in there."

I was numb. I wanted to cry but I was too mad for emotions. At that moment, my only thought was killing that bitch. And as for Malik, I couldn't understand how he could do that to me. I didn't even look at other niggas in the street. And believe me, I had many chances to get some casual dick. But I never fell victim to another nigga's game. I remained faithful to mine. He didn't have to get ass from the next chick because I did everything he wanted. Besides, of all the broads in Queensbridge, dying to give him some pussy, I would have never pictured him going at Reece. I heard that bitch had gonorrhea and was burning dudes all over the hood.

"Chaka, are you still there?"

I collapsed onto the floor, on my brand new carpet, in my brand new Hollyhood apartment and was in utter shock.

"Are you sure Taylor? Because you know Keisha be making

shit up just to gossip."

Of course I knew she was telling me nothing but the truth but my heart didn't want to believe her.

"Chaka, you know I wouldn't lie to you. I told you from day one that Malik was a dog."

She was right, she did warn me. But damn, what the fuck was I supposed to do?

I was fuming so I jumped up from off of the floor and started pacing back and forth through the living room, continually looking out of the window. I don't know what the hell I was looking for but maybe I was hoping I would see him walk into the building with an explanation for everything.

"Yo, I'ma beat Reece's ass when I see that hoe. That's my word."

The phone wasn't even on my ear while I was yelling. I was holding it like a walkie-talkie and just screamed into it. I needed a Newport badly so I marched over to the table and took one out of the box.

"What? Are you stupid?" Taylor asked out of the blue.

"No, I ain't stupid. But I'll tell you who is stupid, that stupid bitch Reece, that's who. And I'ma whoop her stupid ass."

"For what, Chaka? Don't play yourself."

"How am I playing myself? That bitch is fucking my man."

Taylor's callous reaction amped me up even more. After all, I felt I had the right to knock Reece out for violating me. Even if we weren't friends anymore, that bitch should've known better.

"First of all, you don't need to be in the streets fighting over some dick." Taylor began yelling right back at me.

"I'm not fighting over dick Taylor. It's the principle. You just don't go around fucking somebody else's man."

I had hoped my response would set her straight.

"Oh now you sound like a complete asshole. Wasn't you fucking him when he was with somebody else?" She barely paused so I knew she wasn't really expecting me to answer. "Chaka, you in the streets now mama. Ain't no such thing as principles when you dealing with that street life."

"Yeah, whatever."

My facial expression was that of a broken doll but I had to

talk as if I had it all under control.

"Whatever? Check this out little girl, and I'm only gonna say this once, you shouldn't give a fuck if he's fucking the next bitch or not. Dude just furnished your whole apartment and what do you think he did for that skeezer? Nothing. You're the one getting the money, the clothes and a roof over your head. What is Reece getting? Not a damn thing but some dick and a fucking cheeseburger from Jackson Hole. If anything, Reece should hate you because she ain't you."

Taylor was always dropping jewels. The more I thought about what she was saying, the more it made sense.

"Well, why didn't you have to go through this with Supreme?"

"Puhleeze," she laughed. "I went through more than this with him. That nigga had a baby on me by another chick uptown. But I sat back and let him do his thing. As long as Supreme took care of home, why would I care what he did in the streets? Niggas don't want a lady that's gonna be all on his back like a hound. Let him be him and you be you. See, that's the problem with y'all young girls. You don't know how to play this game like a real woman. Just chill the fuck out and act like everything is the same because it still is. He's still with you and if you're fucking him right, he ain't going nowhere."

She continued on, "Anyways, I have to go pick up Junior from school. I promised Supreme that we would go see him today."

"Damn, ain't he all the way up in Elmira?"

I was referring to the notorious maximum security prison in Upstate New York. Not too many motherfuckers wanted to end up in there.

"Yeah, but the bus going up, leaves later on tonight. So, we're going shopping first because he needs some sneakers and toiletries. Then we're on our way for that long ass fucking ride."

"Well, tell Preme I said hi and I miss his crazy ass. Call me when you get back."

"Yup and remember what I said Chiggy, just chill and be easy." Taylor gave me her last two cents before hanging up the phone.

I smiled, fondly remembering the nickname. I hadn't been called Chiggy since getting kicked out of my mother's house. My family called me that when I was a baby. I don't know how it came to be my moniker because it sounded like it should have been used to describe a fat person. Still, I loved it. Hearing Taylor call me by that name made me yearn for my mother. I attempted to dial her telephone number until I heard a knock on the door. Quickly, I forgot all about my mother and Chiggy for that matter. Besides, neither one of them had a place in the world I was living in at that moment.

"That better be my motherfucking girl," I yelled through the door before I opened it.

"Ya got that shit right, Jack." Ta-Ta came in carrying a black plastic bag with Dana and Carmen by her side.

I could tell by the bag that she had just come from the liquor store which was a good thing because I desperately needed a drink.

"Wassup girl? You know we had to come through too," Carmen said.

"Hold it." I put my hand up and stopped all three before they could walk any further into my apartment. "Y'all know you gotta take them shoes off right there."

I pointed toward the closet next to the front door so they knew I meant business. They swiftly got barefoot before walking across my new carpet.

"Damn, the furniture man didn't come yet?" Dana asked.

"No he came, can't you see the couch sitting right there?" I didn't mean to be sarcastic but that was a dumb ass question, especially since there was nothing in the living room.

Ta-Ta walked over to the dining room table and pulled the gallon bottle of Hennessey out of the plastic bag. She must have really wanted to get wasted because she got the one with the handle which meant she wasn't playing around. Carmen headed into the kitchen and grabbed four glasses from off of the dish rack. Even though they were already cleaned, she still rinsed them out before bringing them to the table.

Dana played her part by pulling the two-liter Pepsi, which was the best chaser for Hennessey, out of the refrigerator. We all sat in the chairs surrounding the table and started to get our drink on.

"Don't put too much soda in mine." Dana told Carmen who was playing bartender for the night. "As a matter of fact, I'll take it straight."

"Damn, bitch, you trying to put hair on your chest or something?" Ta-Ta said.

"Chaka, wassa matter with you mami?" Carmen obviously noticed my dazed expression.

"Yo, y'all won't believe the shit I just heard." I realized that I had still been in a state of shock since speaking to Taylor.

The girls knew what I had to say was important because everybody stopped talking instantly.

"I heard Malik is fucking with Reece."

"What?" Ta-Ta shook her head. "See what I mean, niggas ain't shit."

"Oh now we gotta kick some ass out here 'cuz these bitches think shit is a game." Dana's attitude reflected how I really wanted to react.

But despite them being my clique, I still didn't want anybody to know the hurt I felt.

"Nah, I'm just gonna chill. I'm too good to be out there fighting and stuff like that. All he's doing is fucking her anyway. I don't care."

I pretended to be emotionless as I tried to portray the nonchalant attitude that Taylor instilled in me just moments before.

"That's good mama because you don't even need to be making yourself look like a fool out there fighting over that bendeja." Carmen must have reached into her Latin arsenal and used one of the five Spanish words she actually knew.

"Man, let's just play some music and get fucked up. Y'all messing up my drink with all this shit." Dana rummaged through my massive bootleg CD collection before finding her jam. "Oh girl, Luther Vandross is my shit."

"A house is not a home."

She belted out every tune as she sat on the floor in her own little world. With a drink tightly nestled in her right hand, she swung her free hand along with the beat of the song. Forget about Amateur Night at The Apollo, we were witnessing

Amateur Night at Chaka's Crib. Carmen, Ta-Ta and I stayed seated at the table and looked on in laughter.

"Ay Diós, here she goes again," Carmen said. "Oh well, mamacitas, let the night begin."

CHAPTER 11

In retrospect, we should have stayed in after we finished that last bit of Hennessey but looking at the same four walls was fucking up my high. Besides, the furniture man had delivered my living room set so we really didn't need to stay in the house anymore.

It was my suggestion to go outside and walk around. The summer was damn near over so we had to get out as much as possible before the weather got all nasty. Nobody went outside when it was cold because it wasn't any fun except for those days it snowed. We would have snowball fights between the six blocks. They always began innocently enough until somebody got drunk and started shooting after getting hit or dunked in the snow. Leave it up to simple ass niggas to always fuck up a good time.

Malik hadn't gotten home yet and it was already past midnight. Knowing his grimy ass, he was probably with that bitch Reece. I didn't care though. I was about to hit the streets, drunk as hell and ready to flirt. All the girls were just as tipsy so there was no telling where the night was going to lead.

Luckily, I was looking good with my 4-inch Gucci monogrammed sling back sandals. I played it low-key with some jean shorts and a white wife-beater tank. My hair was pulled into a cute ponytail that sat high on my head and swung side to side every time I took a step. My bling was courtesy of the matching gold X and O necklace, bracelet and earring set Malik bought me. That was one thing I couldn't complain about, he kept me looking flossy every day.

We walked onto the hill to see what was popping. It was the same old shit as usual. Other girls were scattered around waiting to catch the attention of some hustler standing on the corner. It was like watching a movie at times. Everything played out for the world to see. With a quick look, you could immediately tell who was fucking who, who already fucked who and who would end up fucking who by the end of the night. In Queensbridge, dick and pussy were conveniently recycled like aluminum cans.

"Yo," a yell came from the group of young dudes on the corner. "Where the weed at? I know y'all got that."

"Nah nigga! We ain't got nothing for you Slime," Ta-Ta said.

"But I'm saying though," the kid yelled again. "I know Chaka got that. What up? I can't get a hi, how you doing, something?"

"Stay in your league young fella." Dana answered him before I could get my rebuttal out. She must have read my mind.

Nothing irked me more than young derelict niggas just starting to hustle. I spent more on shopping for shoes than they made on the first and fifteenth of every month. But it was kind of cute when I thought about how hard they tried. I was that chick in the hood that all the younger guys pictured fucking in a wet dream. They would even tell their girls to try to be more like me. Imitation was the greatest form of flattery and I loved every attempt of duplication.

As we made our way to the benches that were at the very top the hill, we saw Reece and her whorish clique sitting directly across the street. My heart pumped with adrenaline. I tried to remember what Taylor told me but all I wanted to do was put my foot in her ass.

"You see them bitches looking over here, don't you?" We took our seats on the bench and stared right back at them while Carmen stated the obvious.

"Oh, they don't want it tonight. I ain't beat a bitch ass in a long time." Ta-Ta spoke loudly so that her voice was heard by Reece's crew.

They, in turn, put a CD into the small portable radio on the bench next to them. I knew the song was directed toward me once I heard the words pump brazenly from the speakers. They stood up and started dancing around, blatantly singing the lyrics to add a little more salt into my wounded heart.

"So I creep, yeah, keep it on the down-low."

They chanted in their best TLC impressions. Of course, they picked the perfect verse for the occasion and the words pierced right through me. They knew how to get under my skin and were doing it flawlessly.

"Yo, I'm about to go over there and kick that fucking radio right off the bench." My blood was pumping like crazy.

Before I realized that Dana wasn't joining in on the conversation, I peeped her walking toward the benches where Reece's crew had claimed their spot. They were still in their own world listening to the music and completely oblivious to the beast on the loose. She got right up on them before they noticed.

"TURN THIS FUCKING SHIT OFF." Dana kicked the radio and made it tumble hard to the ground.

By the time her leg went up in the air, we had all jumped off of our bench and started running toward them. It was about to go down one way or another and Dana was just the one who felt the need to set it off. I kicked off my sandals and ran barefoot across the street. By default, we knew they had to react to Dana. If they didn't, everybody in the hood would know they were punks and they'd get played out every day.

Dana jumped back and put her hands up ready to fight.

"What? What the fuck y'all gonna do?" Her words spat out with a wail that meant she was in full crazy woman mode.

"Bitch, I know you ain't come over here and do some ill shit." Kia sprang from the bench.

A car screeched to a halting stop as we raced across the street yelling out threats about what would happen once we made our way to them. Dana didn't have to look around, knowing with certainty that as soon as she leapt, we would be right behind her.

"Yeah bitches, y'all was asking to get your asses beat for a while." Ta-Ta lunged toward Kia who was bending over to pick up a bottle.

Before she could grab it, Ta-Ta was on her back. She yoked her up in a headlock and proceeded to drag her to the ground. By that time, both Carmen and Dana had Sheena hemmed up against the brick building while they were both swinging wildly. Carmen was punching her in the face and Dana was throwing sharp body blows that seemed like missiles through her fat ass stomach.

From my peripheral, I saw Reece try to sneak off and make her way down the hill. Before I knew it, I had a ponytail of her box-braids balled up into my fist. When she tried to get away, I felt a few of them pull from the root which made me open my hand wider to grab even more. There was no way I was letting her get away.

Reece screamed out, "Get her off of me."

Her voice only made me angrier. I brought her face down to my knee and continued banging her head against it. With my free hand, I pounded away, caving hard into the center of her shoulder blades.

People started gathering around to watch the fight. Nobody tried to break that shit up though. Shit, we were the entertainment of the night. Fuck the WWF, we had the Battle Royal right there in the hood.

"Oh shit, Chaka is fucking Reece up," shouted an onlooker.

"That ain't shit, look what they doing over there," said another, referring to my friends.

I had gotten Reece on the ground. She caught a few good blows, mostly just scratching my face. A jealous bitch always goes for the pretty girl's face in a fight. Too bad for her though because my scratches would eventually heal but she was going to remember that ass beating for the rest of her miserable life.

I straddled her, pinning her arms to her side with my knees. Since she couldn't move her hands, I had free will to go at it. And I did just that. I blacked out with every punch and pictured her fucking Malik.

Although I didn't fight much, every now and then I had

to let it be known that I wasn't a punk. Before that night, I don't think people really knew my fighting skills at all. They thought I was just a pretty girl who happened to have friends who could fight. But they were mistaken because that night, I had unequivocally proven that I could hold my own as well.

The sounds of sirens snapped me back into reality and the crowd dispersed. My friends had already taken heed and stopped fighting the others. Dana grabbed me up by my shoulders and started pulling me down the hill. The police didn't actually get out of their unmarked car. Instead, they just yelled for us to break it up. It was a girl fight so they knew there wasn't going to be any shooting. Niggas were the ones who didn't know how to fight a fair one anymore. They were quick to pull out guns once one of them started losing. But with girls, everything was personal. I personally wanted to beat her ass and so I did.

We ran quickly down the hill, laughing and slapping fives at our most recent victory.

"Stupid bitches," Ta-Ta yelled out loud enough for the whole projects to hear. "Y'all ain't shit."

Reece and her crew managed to scrape it together and started heading toward their block. When they got further away from us, they yelled out threats about what they were going to do the next time they caught one of us by ourselves. That was typical behavior of bitches who just lost a fight – talk about what they will do instead of what they just got done to them.

"What the fuck ever," Carmen hollered back. "Come on and do it now mama. Y'all wait until the police come to start talking shit."

"Keep it moving. Keep it moving." The police slowly cruised beside us with their windows rolled down halfway.

"I'm saying though." Dana's rude ass jumped frog right up to the driver's side door. "Why you ain't following them?"

"Because by the looks of it, they aren't going to try to fight anymore tonight." The cop cracked a smile that instantly caught my attention. "Now go home and don't make us have to come back out here."

If I remember correctly, he even threw me a quick wink of the eye.

The police drove off but not before warning us that we'd be arrested if we were still there when they returned. Honestly, they could have kept their reprimands for somebody else because we were done for the night. We did our thing and we knew it would be the talk of the hood for days to come.

I prayed Malik wouldn't find out. I knew if word had gotten back to him, he would have flipped about me being out there acting a fucking fool. He had a thing about his lady staying out of the streets whenever he wasn't around. But, shit, he made me the way I was so who was he to get upset? He should have thought about that before he stuck his dick into that nasty whore anyway.

We went back up to my apartment for a little while. As we lit a blunt, we held a verbal instant replay of everything that had just happened.

"Yo, once Dana kicked the radio off the bench, I knew it was on." Ta-Ta busted out laughing as she inhaled a long pull of the Chocolate Thai weed.

"That was crazy! Damn, I ain't fight in forever," I said.

We laughed and continued talking. Before we knew it, it was four in the morning by the time they were walking out my door. Just to be on the safe side, they all walked home together so there was no chance of anybody getting jumped. Reece and her crew were so mad about getting their asses beat that there was no telling how they would retaliate.

It was almost day break and Malik still hadn't made it home. If it wasn't Reece that night, he had obviously found someone else to fuck. I couldn't fight the whole hood and it wouldn't have made a difference if I did. He was still out in the streets and I was still in the house by myself.

That night, I had wished Bandit was there with me. At least that way, I wouldn't have been alone. But I had gotten so used to it that by then, loneliness had become my best friend. Too bad for me, a ghetto girl fight in the hood didn't change a thing. And it surely didn't bring Malik home.

But I ain't gonna lie, it made me feel a whole hell of a lot better. Even if that feeling was only temporary.

CHAPTER 12

The cold steel pressed against my temple jolted me out of my sleep. I didn't have a chance to fully open my eyes before the comforter was pulled off and thrown to the floor. As I looked up, Malik was standing over me with a pistol resting on the side of my face.

"So you want to be out there fighting like a typical project bitch, huh?" His voice was grim.

"Malik, what are you doing? I wasn't..."

"Now you gonna lie? Bitch, you was out there acting a fool last night. Fighting and shit, huh? You went against the grain this time."

"Malik, what are you doing? She started with me."

"I don't wanna hear none of that. Stand the fuck up and strip."

I quickly obliged by pulling off my t-shirt and stepping out of my panties.

"So when I let you out the house, you wanna act stupid, right?" He pointed the gun directly at me from his spot on the edge of the bed.

I had no idea what he was going to do and that made me panic even more. Besides a push or a slap here and there, he hadn't beaten me since that day at his mother's house. I knew he would flip if he found out about the fight but I didn't expect his response to be that extreme.

"Now, your dumb ass ain't going nowhere," he shouted.

That was the first time he had raised his voice since waking me up with the gun to my head. However, I had learned not to talk back to him. When he was in that phase, I couldn't get through to him even if I tried.

"Let's go." He grabbed the nape of my neck and shoved me forward.

I walked slowly out of the bedroom. My first thought was that he was going to throw me out of the house. The idea of running through the hood butt naked made me drop to my knees, too embarrassed to face that possibility.

"Malik, no. I can't go out there." I reached my arms out and tried to hold onto the walls, a doorknob or something to keep me planted.

"Get the fuck up and get in the living room bitch," he said.

When I got into the living room, there was a girl sitting on the couch who I had never seen before. Since I knew everybody in the hood, I knew for a fact that she wasn't from Queensbridge. The girl sat there quietly as if Malik's actions were not surprising to her at all.

"So, you wanna be out there fighting 'cause you think I'm fucking somebody, huh?"

"No Malik, she was messing with me. I ain't do nothing to her."

I had no idea what he was doing or why there was a stranger watching everything go down.

Malik took his belt off and gave the girl his gun. She kept it pointed directly at me. He grabbed me by the arms despite my twists as I made every attempt to loosen myself. Pulling me over to the radiator, he held my two hands together and tied them tight with the belt. He then tied the belt to the pipes so I couldn't move.

"Bitch, I ain't gotta hide nothing from you. If I wanna fuck somebody, I'ma fuck them right in front of you." He had a crazed look on his face. "I give you everything you want and you go out there and fight a bitch over some shit you heard in the streets?"

"I didn't hear nothing. Malik, what are you doing?" I tried to squirm my hands from the tight belt. "Let me go."

"Nah, you gonna sit right there and see I ain't got nothing

to hide from you."

Malik looked over to the girl who had put the gun on the coffee table. She stood up and started to undress. She was dark-skinned and had her hair pulled back into a short greasy looking ponytail. Her face looked like she had been in too many fights with dark black circles under her eyes and old scratch marks on her cheeks. But when she stood there naked, her body was flawless. Her breasts were plump and stood erect as if they were pointing directly at me. Her stomach was flat and her tiny waist led to an ass that would rival a video chick.

She got down doggy-style on my carpet and opened her butt cheeks for Malik. Before my eyes, I watched him pull his hardening dick from the zipper opening of his pants.

"What are you doing?" I screamed. "Malik, what the fuck is going on?"

"I'ma show you what I do if I wanna fuck somebody. Bitch I made you. I ain't gotta hide shit from your young stupid ass."

He grabbed the girl's hips from behind and thrust, raw dog, into her asshole. She let out a moan before starting to move back and forth with his rhythm. He fucked her like a wild animal. The mere sight of it made me sick. So much so, that I couldn't control the vomit that sprouted from my mouth as it made its way up my throat. By that point, I had ceased pleading with him. It felt like the more I begged him to stop, the more excited he grew which inevitably turned her on.

From his quickened pace, I could tell he was about to cum. He took his dick out of her ass and on cue, the girl turned around to catch every last drop. Malik let out a groan before ejaculating all over her face and hair. She laughed while she licked it from the corners of her mouth.

My cries were without sound. I was too shocked to let out anything audible. I couldn't believe he could do that to me.

The girl taunted me by flapping her tongue in my face with his cum still dripping down her mouth and onto her breasts. Malik took about a hundred dollars out of his pocket and threw it on her along with a wet dishcloth he grabbed from the kitchen.

"Now, get the fuck outta here," he said.

She purred like a cat in heat. "All right Daddy."

The girl got up and put her clothes back on. The nasty bitch didn't even clean her ass. She wiped the cum from her face, looked back at me and laughed.

"Play your fucking position and get out my house you once a month bleeding bitch." Malik's tone was stern without raising his voice.

She took heed and didn't look back. After grabbing the money, she was gone within seconds. He locked the door and looked down at me but I couldn't react. I was in complete disarray.

"Now think about that before you go back out there fighting some bitches because you think I'm fucking one of them," he said. "That's how I treat bitches, just like I did that smut bitch. You fighting a bitch that I treat like shit and you getting everything. I knew I shouldn't have fucked with your little stupid ass anyway. Now you lay there and don't say a word until I tell you to talk."

He walked to the bathroom and I heard him turn the water on and get into the shower. I was still at a loss as to what he was going to do to me. I kept trying to loosen up the belt but I couldn't. All those stupid ass self-defense classes I took when I was younger didn't help me when I really needed it.

I replayed Malik's proclamation in my head, "*Bitch I made you.*"

He did make me, didn't he? What would I do if he threw me out? I didn't have anywhere else to go. My mother's house was out for the question. Although she and I had managed to patch things back up, I couldn't go back to living under her roof with her rules. I was too grown for that.

The thought of my future without Malik made me cry harder than being forced to watch him fuck some random chick right in front of me. The truth was that I had nowhere else to go. All I had was right there, where the stench of sex mixed with my own vomit circulated throughout. I was determined to never go back to being a nobody.

I cried out in despair but my cries fell on deaf ears. By then, Malik was already out of the shower and asleep in our bed. I felt like Bandit probably felt when he was tied to the radiator. And just as easy as it was for Malik to get rid of Bandit, he made it perfectly clear that he could do the same thing to me. It was at that point I knew, somehow, he would.

CHAPTER 13

Malik and I never spoke about the actions of that night. I wanted to forget they ever happened and he spoiled me with enough lavish gifts to redeem himself for what he did. I actually looked forward to the make-ups because that's when he was the old Malik who I fell in love with in the first place.

Although I wasn't allowed to go outside for a while, except to the store or the laundromat, Malik finally gave in and slowly things got back to normal. By normal, I mean, his attentive methods of apologizing had gotten less and his need to roam the streets had become more prevalent.

Of course the knowledge of him fucking Reece was still fresh in my mind but he made sure I never had the courage to ask him about another woman ever again. And since I didn't want a repeat of his forceful show of authority, I never did.

Time and time again I weighed the pros and cons of being in that relationship. Malik really did have a lot of good characteristics even if I was the only one who witnessed them. We had fun together on those occasions when he wasn't beating my ass. I remember him buying matching mountain bikes for us. His was blue and mine was red. We would glide through the projects like JFK and Jackie O but without the whole Texas assassination and shit. Sometimes we'd even make the ten minute trek over to Roosevelt Island and pop a bottle of Moët by the water.

Nobody saw the many occasions when we'd pack a lunch and picnic in Central Park. Well, except for the one time we had sex under the picnic sheet in broad daylight. Every single person in the park stood there and watched us, pointing and giggling at the two love birds that couldn't get enough of each other. It was those rare glimpses into his heart that kept me around hoping one day he would be that person again.

So despite what people told me about Malik being a no-good this and a no-good that, I was still in love with him. He showed me things that I had never seen before. With him I had money, power and respect – the three things I never had without him. As long as he gave me what I needed, I would never stop giving him everything he wanted.

I was asleep and woke up to the darkness of my bedroom. I touched the spot where Malik slept and felt nothing. By the time on the alarm clock next to my bed, it was already six in the morning and that nigga still wasn't home. It seemed like every other day, he'd stay out and barely make it in before the sun. Complaining would be useless or could even lead to being tied up again so I rolled over and laid there looking up at the ceiling hoping he'd come home.

I heard the keys jingle, opening the door to the apartment. When Malik entered, there was another person with him whose voice sounded very familiar.

"Yeah man, it's cool, you can sleep on the couch," Malik said.

Mystery man replied, "Thanks, I'm only in town for a few days. I was staying with my sister but she got too many kids running around her house."

I raked my brain to match a face and name to that voice but I couldn't figure it out. Damn, I thought it sounded like Jamere but I knew he had moved to Atlanta so it couldn't have been him.

"Where should I put my bags?" Mystery voice asked.

I knew that sound from anywhere. It was Jamere. My initial reaction was to run into the living room and straight into his arms but I knew Malik would flip if he saw how excited I was for another man. Besides, I was only wearing a t-shirt and panties with no plans on getting up and putting more clothes on. It was too early in the damn morning and ain't nobody had time for that.

They spoke for about ten minutes while I tried my hardest to eavesdrop on their conversation. I couldn't wait to talk to Jamere in the morning. After all, the last time he saw me, I was looking like a battered housewife.

Malik came into the room and walked quietly to his dresser. He took out a pair of boxers and a t-shirt, I knew because I kept one eye opened, watching him while I pretended to be asleep. He walked out of the bedroom and into the bathroom which confused me until I heard the shower water start running.

My mother always warned me that if a man comes home late and the shower is the first place he runs, then he was probably out fucking all night. I guess the saying is true, *"mother knows best"*.

The water shut off and instantly Malik was dressed and hopping into bed.

"Six o'clock in the morning, huh?" My eyes stayed glued to the ceiling as I spoke.

"I thought you was sleeping," he said.

"You thought I was sleep or you hoped I was sleep?"

"Chaka not tonight, aight. Damn, I was with Jamere and the boys."

I could tell he was lying because his alibi seemed too rehearsed. But once he turned away and gave me the cold shoulder, I immediately knew that I had pissed him off. He used to get into our bed and hug on me but lately he hadn't touched me at all. Shit, I just wanted him to want me again.

I reached over his body and placed my hand on his dick. Gently, I caressed and played with him until he started getting hard. I knew all the tricks to get him going – tickle the head, softly cup the balls – I knew how to pleasure my man better than any other chick could.

Once his hips started humping along with mine, I knew he was ready. I undressed and mounted his fully erect dick. My pussy was wet as usual allowing him to enter as smooth as butter.

"Don't be so loud. Jamere is out there."

His warning went through one ear and out of the other. When I was in *fuck mode'* nothing else mattered. He started slapping me on my ass which made me move faster and harder. Once I spun around on his dick and gave him the reverse cowgirl position, I knew I had him.

"Aghh," he screamed.

From the sound, I knew he came. Although, he never took much time to make sure I had an orgasm, I was glad I could still satisfy him. Sex was the weapon I used to keep him. Whatever he wanted, I did. If he wanted anal sex, I was the first one to grab the oil and get to lubricating. If he felt like getting a blow job while he watched the Super Bowl, I would slob until the winning touchdown was scored. There were times when I was embarrassed to partake in the many sexually deviant acts he demanded. But if I didn't do them, then I knew somebody else would. And if I was going to keep my man, I had to perform in a way that he never had a reason to look elsewhere.

"I love you, Chako," he softly said after reviving himself from his post-cum stupor.

"I love you too Baby." I was beaming inside, happy that he called me Chako again.

Regardless of what Malik did, I knew I would always love him. Honestly, in my own little way, I probably still do.

CHAPTER 14

The ringing phone startled me out of a deep comatose-like sleep. It was only ten in the morning and way too early for somebody to have the audacity to be calling my damn phone.

"Hello," I slurred groggily into the receiver.

"Chaka, are you asleep?"

My mother had no remorse about calling me early in the morning practically every day. She thought it was a sin to sleep past nine.

"Mommy, you know I'm sleep, what's up?"

"Nothing, I'm at work now and I just wanted to call you, that's all."

"You always wanna call me when I'm sleeping."

"Well anyway, where's your bum of a boyfriend?"

"Mommy, please, not today. Did you just call me to start talking about that again?"

"And so what if I did?" My mother responded without the least bit of shame. "But no, I didn't. I was calling to see if you wanted to go to church with me on Sunday? Pastor said he would really like to see you at a service and Lord knows you need to be there."

My mother had started going to church years before and it helped her get her life together. The pastor was a fly, pimp-looking motherfucker who was always decked out in the latest fashions. He drove a silver BMW while most of the congregation was scrounging money together to catch a train to get to their minimum wage jobs. He preached from the pulpit wearing alligator shoes and an ice boulder on his pinky finger. In the winter, he stayed minked down with full length coats and matching chinchilla hats. Every summer, dude was wearing ostrich and crocodile sandals. Shit, his footwear alone was enough to make the endangered species list.

Around the way, we called him Reverend Money Bags. I gave him his props though – everybody had a hustle and his just happened to be the church. At least he gave the ghetto dwellers like my mother, something to believe in and there was no way anybody could ever knock him for that.

"Yeah, Ma, I'll go. But really, it's Thursday. Did you have to call me now? Bye."

I hung up the phone before she had a chance to say anything else. My biggest pet peeve in life has always been people waking me up before noon when I have absolutely no place to go and nothing to do.

On the other hand, I was happy that my mother and I were friends again. She was slowly but surely learning to respect me as a woman. We did Saturdays together, meaning we'd get our hair done, have lunch or go shopping. I didn't go to my old house that much anymore. Daddy still wasn't speaking to me and on the rare occasion when he did, it wasn't like it used to be.

When my mother found out about Malik, she initially threatened to call the police hoping that would finally get me out from under him. But I called her bluff knowing she was all talk. Deep down, my mother was still a street woman so she knew what time it was. Malik was my sponsor and no matter what she said, she would never fuck that up for her baby girl.

I tossed around in the bed constantly changing positions trying desperately to go back to sleep. I even tried to pull the comforter over my head to block the sunlight but that didn't work either.

"Fuck," I yelled.

Since my body wasn't going to allow me to catch any more

shut-eye, I reached over to the nightstand and grabbed a cigarette. No face washing, no teeth brushing, no breakfast eating. My first thing in the morning routine consisted of taking a few pulls from a Newport to completely wake me up.

I noticed Malik was already gone which didn't surprise me in the least bit. He was never there when I went to bed and was seldom there when I woke up. I heard some noise in the bathroom and was actually shocked that he hadn't made his way out the door yet.

Patiently I waited for him to get out of the bathroom because I had to pee like a racehorse. He was taking too damn long so I jumped off of the bed, still butt ass naked from our tryst the night before and made my way to the bathroom. I flung the door open without knocking and was paralyzed by the sight in front of me. Looking at his face was futile because I could tell by the size of the dick that it wasn't Malik walking out of the shower. I was looking at Mandingo in the flesh. His dick was far from being rock hard and it still hung all the way down to the middle of his thigh.

Believe me, I know. I still think about that shit every now and again.

"Oh shit, Jamere, I'm sorry." The words mumbled from my mouth that fell agape at the vision before me.

My body stayed motionless as I stared back at the Adonis-like statue. I had completely forgotten that Jamere spent the night and there he was standing in my bathroom totally naked.

That's when it hit me – I was naked too.

Finally, I closed the bathroom door and darted back to my room. But it was too late. We both had visuals that neither one of us would ever forget.

Jamere knocked on the door before sticking his head through the cracked opening.

"Chak you all right?"

"Oh my God, get out of here." I spoke from under the comforter where I had sought my hiding place.

He walked in with nothing but a towel wrapped around his waist. His dick still poked out slightly from the gape going down the middle. My pussy got wet just at the sight of it.

"Jamere, I forgot you were here. I am so sorry."

Of course, I wasn't being completely honest. The only thing I was sorry about was the fact that I had never really noticed how sexy he was before then.

"So what's up with you?" He copped a squat at the foot of my bed. Apparently, he didn't give a fuck that we were both naked.

Since moving to Atlanta, he had put on a little weight but it looked good on him. He had also cut his curly hair and was sporting a baldy with hints of gray in his goatee. Damn, he was finer than a motherfucker to me. At that moment, I didn't give a shit if Malik walked in on us or not.

"How's Atlanta?" I finally found the courage to poke my head out from under the covers.

"It's cool. Business is really good so I just opened another store."

"You opened a store?" I was astonished. Before then, I never knew anybody who actually owned a business.

"Yeah, I gotta make this money legal somehow."

I heard what he was saying but it made no sense to me. I was too busy living for the moment to care about building something for the future. Malik would always be making money and I'd always be set. Everything I needed was locked away in a safe. Fuck a job. My employer was Malik and being with him was hard work so I deserved every penny.

"When are you coming to visit?"

"Visit where? I ain't going down there with all them country people."

After all, I was a city girl and there was no way I was about to be chucking and jiving with those chitterling eating slow ass motherfuckers.

"I mean, what do you got going on up here that's so important? You need a change."

While he spoke, the only thought crossing my mind was the sexy ass man sitting a few inches away from me as I lay naked under the covers. Who gave a fuck about some life in Atlanta?

"Yeah, yeah, yeah Jamere, now get out of here." I slapped my hand on his back but kept my other hand on my chest to keep the comforter in place.

"Remind me to leave my number with you so you can call me for anything," he said. "And I mean anything, Chak."

Jamere stood up and walked toward the door. Before leaving the room, he stopped and bent over to kiss my forehead. I reached up to hug him and the comforter slipped down revealing my hardened nipples. It didn't matter because I was hugging him real tight with my titties pressed against the hairs on his chest. I couldn't help but kiss his lips. It was like they were just calling out to me. He then raised the stakes and gently licked the corners of my mouth.

There we were, in the bed that my man and I shared, and neither one of us gave a fuck. Jamere traced the brown circles around my breast with his tongue. He was sensual with every touch, much different than anything I had experienced with Malik. I wanted him inside of me so badly.

"Come down south with me Chaka," he whispered, suspending our moment of sexual bliss.

"No, don't stop, I'll go anywhere. Just please don't stop."

Jamere pulled away from me just as I was about to suction my mouth around his dick.

"No, get dressed. I'll be in the living room," he said before walking out the door.

"Damn," I yelled. "What a way to start my day."

First I tried to sleep and that got cut short. Then I tried to get fucked and that didn't work out either. That day wasn't off to a good start to say the least.

Finally, I got up and went straight to the bathroom. Embarrassed by Jamere's rejection, I wanted to get the fuck out of the house quickly without facing him. I jumped in the shower only to realize there was no hot water, yet another sign of a fucked up day.

The water was like ice but I managed to get wet only when I absolutely needed to rinse off. I could have boiled some on the stove and used it but then I would have had to go into the kitchen and risk bumping into Jamere again.

Within a few minutes, I was bathed and out of the icebox. I opened the medicine cabinet to get some tooth paste to take care of that morning tart baking in my mouth. When I took the paste out, I noticed a bag of dope behind it. That was strange and completely out of place. We were always very careful not to leave drugs lying around the house. The police could pop up at anytime and all they needed to see was the slightest hint of drug activity. Therefore, we always kept the drugs, the money and the two guns Malik had, locked away in a safe. The police would never notice the hole we made in the wall behind the cabinet because it was covered with wall paper. It was the perfect stash spot.

On instinct, I grabbed the bag and knew from its weight that it had been opened. It was only a twenty but by then, I had bagged up enough drugs to know how much it should have weighed without needing a scale. I flushed the remainder of the heroin down the toilet and didn't give a fuck whose it was.

Jamere must have been in there sniffing dope, I thought. He was the only one, besides me, who was in the house. It couldn't have been Malik because I would have known if he was tapping the product. So the only culprit was Jamere, the same person that was fronting like he was doing so well in Atlanta. In reality, he wasn't anything more than a fucking junkie. I was so glad I didn't give his dopefiend ass some pussy.

I walked back into my room and didn't mention anything to Jamere who was sitting on the couch in the living room. When Malik got home, I'd let him know that his friend had to get the fuck out of our house.

My outfit for the day was on some Chuck-Chill-Out shit and consisted of a plain white t-shirt, light gray sweats and white Air Force Ones. With the way my day was going, I wasn't in the mood to get all cute.

I jetted toward the front door, placed a spare key on the table and told Jamere to lock up if he went out. Once I got downstairs it dawned on me that I had just left my apartment in the hands of a drug addict. I almost wanted to run back up but in a way, I still trusted Jamere. Regardless of the drugs, he would have never done me dirty.

The air outside was extremely humid and it wasn't even noon yet. I pulled my sweatpants up to my knees to give my legs a little breathing room and headed toward Ta-Ta's block. As I crossed the street, I was nearly run over by Malik's car.

BEEP. The car's horn blared loudly. As I approached, he rolled the driver's side window down half-way.

"What's up babe?" I asked. "Where are you going?"

Immediately I noticed how sweaty he looked. Even though the humidity was on full blast, it wasn't hot enough for him to be sweating like an African. His eyes were wide and instead of focusing his attention on me, he kept looking all around the car and continuously checking his rearview mirror.

"Hello, Earth to Malik, what's wrong with you?"

"Nah, nothing. I just took care of something, that's all. Where you heading?" Although he answered me, he was still too preoccupied with everything else going on around us.

"I'm going to Ta-Ta's house, where are you going?" I sensed he was trying to get rid of me.

"All right, I'll be around."

He drove off before I could say another word. Lately he seemed to always be on the move some damn where. Even when we bagged up, he would be fidgeting all around and talking mad loud. He was fucking the weight up and not putting enough dope in the bags. Something was wrong with him but I couldn't figure out what it was.

Malik's demeanor only added to my level of aggravation which at that point was nearing an all time high. Since my mood was shot, my whole plans for the day had changed. I no longer felt like going to Ta-Ta's house and dealing with the crazy shit that went on over there. Actually, I was wondering what the hell Jamere was doing in the crib while I was gone. I was still somewhat nervous about leaving him in there after discovering that he was on drugs. So, I turned around and went back upstairs.

When I got into the apartment it seemed as though he had already left. But, his bags were still in the closet so I figured he'd be back later.

I checked the jewelry box in my room to make sure my shit was still there. The first thing I looked for was my 3-ct diamond tennis bracelet that Malik bought me for Christmas. He copped it from a crackhead but that didn't matter to me. When I took it to get appraised, the shit was still three carats whether it was from Jacob the Jeweler or the local pawn shop.

The bracelet was safely in its spot.

Quickly, I took an inventory of all my other jewelry and nothing seemed to be out of place. My diamond studs, platinum baguette ring and gold herringbone chain were all there, just the way I had left them.

My next concern was the safe. Although Jamere didn't know about it, I still needed to check that shit out too. We had the wall paper taped inconspicuously on the side so that the opening was camouflaged in with the rest of the wall. Nobody else knew the combination except for me and Malik. Even with that in mind, I still wanted to check it just to be on the safe side.

Those fucking combination locks got on my damn nerves especially when I was already in panic mode. Perhaps that's why I was always late to class because I could never get the fucking school locker open quick enough.

Four to the left, twelve to the right, I finally got the damn thing to crack.

I noticed there was only one gun in the safe which wasn't strange because Malik probably had the nine-millimeter with him. But then I realized there weren't any drugs inside either. That was kind of peculiar until I remembered the last time I checked, we were low and due to re-up. Malik had probably found somebody to buy the little bit we had left. That was a good thing because the bottom of the bag was always bullshit product anyway.

The only thing left was the money. I grabbed the stacks and sat on the floor to count it. It was normally a big bundle so I took my time.

By my count, there was only $5,000 which couldn't have been right so I counted that shit again. When I tallied it for the second time, it came up to exactly $4,980. There was supposed to close to $11,000 in that pile so how I kept coming up with less than that wasn't making any sense to me. It couldn't have been Malik because I knew he would never take that much money without telling me. Instantly, I knew who took it. Jamere was the only motherfucker who was ever alone in my house. He must've broken into the safe. In my mind, there was no one else who could have done that.

My heart was racing as I ran to the closet and pulled Jamere's bags out. I ransacked his shit looking for my loot. His clothes were thrown all over the floor and every pocket to every jean was turned inside out. There wasn't a red cent anywhere. I figured he must have had the money on him and was walking around the projects spending it on drugs just like a fucking fiend.

I beeped Malik with a 911 code so that he knew it was urgent. We had to catch Jamere before he spent up our money. The next call I made was to Ta-Ta. I knew no matter what, she had my back. I wanted her to go outside and look for him too. The more eyes we had on the street, the easier it would be to find his drugging ass. If I saw that nigga, I promised myself, I would shoot him in both kneecaps.

Malik was taking too long to call back and Ta-Ta wasn't answering her phone. Waiting around was killing me so I threw the money back into the safe and didn't bother locking it up. Instead, I just put the tape on the wall and headed out the door to find Jamere on my own.

But I wouldn't get far though. The terror that waited outside of my apartment door was much worse than anything I had yet experienced. And silly me, I was walking right into it.

CHAPTER 15

BAM
I felt a blow to the side of my head right next to my temple. The punch hit me so hard that I lost my balance and literally saw stars. Before I could regain my composure, I was pushed back into the house and thrown onto the floor. When I looked up, I saw three dudes standing over me. They were all wearing hoodies so I really couldn't see their faces. But what I did see was a shiny nickel plated barrel pointed right at me.

"Bitch don't scream or I'll blow your fucking head off." The guy holding the gun knelt down and squished it into my cheek. "Stay the fuck on the floor and don't move."

From the corner of my eye, I saw the other two brolic niggas frantically looking through all the rooms in the apartment.

"Yo, he ain't here," one of them yelled out.

When I finally heard him speak, I turned to face him head on.

"Yeah bitch, look at me. You know who the fuck I am," he said.

I knew by his voice that it was Monty, the kid we did business with from Far Rockaway. But why he was in my house wilding out was beyond me. I didn't know what the hell was going on.

"Where's your bitch ass man?" The goon with the gun still had the shit pointed at my face.

I stayed mute.

"Oh, you don't wanna say nothing? Yo Gee, smack that bitch again," Monty said.

SLAM – the second blow caught me in my right jaw just in case I thought for one second that shit wasn't real. After I figured out it was Monty and his Far Rockaway niggas, I knew my chances of walking out of there alive were slim to none.

I heard the dresser in my room being opened and the drawers toppled over onto the floor. I wanted to cry but I wouldn't give those sons of bitches the satisfaction of seeing me get emotional.

I peered down the hallway into my bedroom where the door was opened. My mattress was overturned and flung to the floor. I couldn't figure out what Malik did to make them go crazy but I wanted to tell them that whatever they were looking for damn sure wasn't in my bedroom.

"Yo, beep your man." Monty picked the phone up from off of the end table and threw it, hitting me square in the middle of my face.

I heard my nose crack and blood began gushing out before the phone fell to the floor. I knew Monty had Malik's beeper number but he didn't know the number to my house. So when I beeped him, I put in a bogus callback and prayed he wouldn't notice. They already had me and I wasn't about to let them get the man I loved too.

"What do y'all want? Why are you doing this Monty?" I finally uttered through the blood that was leaking from my nose and into my mouth.

"Shut up bitch. You don't ask no questions," Gee yelled.

He began to approach me before Monty stopped his hand in mid-air. In a way, I was ready for him to hit me so he could have ended the whole shit right then and there. Actually, I was mentally prepared for them to shoot me by then. Waiting to die seemed far worse than simply dying.

"You know y'all fucked up right?" Monty said.

Still, I had no idea what he was talking about. The other two were rummaging through the apartment. One of them was in the kitchen and the other was going through the hallway closet. I let out a sigh when I remembered I left the safe open.

I was so vexed when I thought Jamere took the money that I ran out of the apartment without ever locking it back up. There was at least five thousand dollars in there and if they found it, I'd be left with nothing. Distraction was the only card I had left to play.

"I don't know what you're talking about Monty. What happened?" I strained my ears to hear if muscle man in the kitchen had reached the cabinet yet.

"You don't know what happened? Don't play me like I'm stupid, bitch. You know your man took twenty stacks from me and never came back with my work."

Twenty thousand fucking dollars? He couldn't have been serious. There must have been some type of mistake. I began to play the whole scenario out in my head.

First of all, Malik got his own money so why would he have to rob some niggas from broke ass Far Rockaway? And second of all, if that shit was true, then why hadn't I seen a dime of that money?

I started to feel as though Malik not only double-crossed those cats but he also betrayed me in the process. Instantly, I was overcome with rage. I no longer gave a damn about being held at gunpoint while my apartment was being demolished. I only cared that I didn't get a cut of the so-called money.

But of course I had to front like I had everything under control. I couldn't let on to those niggas that my man cut my throat just like he cut theirs. If I had even given them an inkling of a thought, they would have known my weakness and used it against me.

"Monty, I don't know nothing about all this. There gotta be a mistake." My tone was sincere and almost apologetic.

It would have made no sense to give dude a smart mouth and risk adding fuel to his fire.

Monty's eyes never looked away from me. His gaze was steady and pierced through to my soul. I tried to avert his attention away from the frightened expression on my face. He sat on the couch with the gun in his right hand waiting for me to even look like I was going to try to make a move. He reminded me of the Grim Reaper with his black hood, black jeans, black boots and one black leather glove. I wondered what exactly was going through his sick ass brain. I mean, what does a nigga think about right before he kills somebody?

I could still hear the other two stooges knocking shit around in the apartment.

"What the fuck is this, bitch?" Gee yelled from the kitchen.

DAMN, I immediately knew his question could have only meant that he found the safe with my little five thousand dollars in it. At that point, that was the only money I had left to my name. I could have shot my own damn self for not locking the safe before I left.

"Yo, I thought you didn't have no money in the house. You little lying bitch." Gee walked out of the kitchen with my stacks in his hand.

I stayed speechless and tried my hardest to remain void of any emotion.

"So what else you got around this motherfucker?" Monty took the money from Gee and threw it at me.

I didn't say a word but every macabre thought imaginable ran through my head.

Pull the fucking trigger already. FUCK IT. My life ain't worth shit anyway.

I peeped the third goon come out of the bedroom with all of my jewelry in his hand. I knew I'd never see that stuff again but all I could do was sit there and watch.

"Ayo, that's it?" Monty turned to his partners and asked.

"Yeah, unless she got something smashed in her pussy, there ain't nothing else. But I'll definitely check her shit if you want, my nigga. This bird brain bitch always thought she was too cute anyway. Let me see how good that pussy really taste."

Gee's ghoulish snarl revealed a yellow chipped canine tooth. As he got closer to me, the malice in his face grew even scarier. He was like the big bad wolf and was ready to eat me alive.

"Nah," Monty said, "that won't be necessary. This bitch is washed up anway. We out."

Relief passed through my body like the great white hope as they all turned and started walking toward the door. At that moment, I didn't give a fuck about the crib, the money or Malik. I was only happy to know I was going to live to see another day. My joy quickly came to a halt when Monty turned back around and walked toward me with the gun still in his gloved right hand.

"Chaka, tell that nigga that we'll be back for our shit and next time you won't be so lucky." Monty whispered cryptically into my ear while he knelt down and kissed me on the cheek.

As he rose, I saw his right hand come down with a horrific force. It reminded me of an eclipse with the gun's black shadow glooming over me. With a furiously swift movement of his wrist, my face contorted and jolted to the side as the barrel of the gun connected with my left temple. I literally heard my ear drum pop until all that was left was a loud stinging persistent ringing sound.

Everything after that was a blur. My knees gave out and my upper body plummeted to the floor. I laid there and watched the last flicker of light go out and then there was nothing but darkness – darkness and that fucking ringing in my ear.

CHAPTER 16

My head throbbed like a marching band performing in the Macy's Thanksgiving Day Parade. I tried desperately to open my eyes but I couldn't find the strength.

"Where am I?" I asked but got no response.

That damn ringing in my ear continued even louder. I tried to remember why my head was hurting and why my body ached but my brain wasn't registering any recollection whatsoever. I heard voices looming around me but I couldn't see any faces. Although I wanted to look, my eyelids felt like they weighed a ton. The voices were immediately recognizable – my mother and Taylor were in the room.

What are they doing here? Why isn't anybody answering my questions?

"She's been like this for three days." I heard my mother talking.

"Mommy, what's going on?"

Still nobody answered me.

"What did the doctors say?" Taylor said.

"They just said she had blunt trauma to her head." I could

tell by the cracking in her voice that my mother was on the verge of an emotional breakdown. "I spoke to Jamere and he said he was coming in the house to get his clothes, because you know he was staying with them for a couple of days. He said when he got there, the door was wide open. When he walked in, the place was trashed and my baby was lying there like this. God only knows how long she was there. The doctor said if it would've been any longer, Oh God, I can't even think about it. Lord Jesus, give me strength."

"Don't cry," I yelled. *"Mommy, I'm all right."*

It was useless, they still couldn't hear me.
"And where is Malik now?" Taylor said.
"That little black son of a bitch. Lord, excuse my language, but ain't nobody heard near word from that bastard." My mother words were full of disgust.

Damn, I remember now, they were looking for Malik to get the money. That's right, he stole some money. And then he hit me with the gun. No, Malik didn't hit me it was the other guy. Malik's friend. Well it ain't his friend no more. I mean it used to be but then they blamed him for taking some money. It's too confusing for me. I can't get my thoughts clear. My head feels so cloudy and heavy. I can't think.

"I told her to stay away from his tired ass. Now look. You know he done heard what happened, because it's all over the projects already, Debra. And he couldn't even come to make sure she was still alive." Taylor sucked her teeth and I could picture her rolling her hazel eyes.
Their voices began to drift off until I couldn't hear them anymore. I had hoped it was just a bad dream and I would wake up to find everything back to normal.

Yeah, I thought, *maybe when I wake up.*

Somehow I finally managed to slowly open my eyes. At first, I still couldn't focus because my vision was blurred.

There seemed to be two of everything in the room. I could see my mother asleep on the chair at the side of my bed with a white sheet draped across her small body. I looked out of the window at the light piercing through the blinds from the moon that shone brightly outside. The only sound I could make out were the beeps from the machines around my bed.

As I raised my head to sit up, I felt wires and tape all over me. There was an IV going into my left arm from a clear bag of fluid that was half empty. My body still ached and my head felt heavy. I reached up and felt my tangled hair matted up like some Brooklyn pickaninny bitch. There was also a bald spot on the left side of my head. I touched the place where my hair used to be and there was a hard knot beneath a mountain of gauze pads.

"Mommy." I was trying to speak loud enough to wake her but the only sound that came out of my dry chapped lips was a muffled whimper.

"MA." I tried again, straining my vocal cords even more.

Her eyes sprung open and I saw a smile appear on her face that I had never seen before. She quickly threw the sheet off of her and leaned close to my bed.

"Chiggy, you're awake. Hi baby girl. How are you feeling?" Her face beamed as she gently stroked my forehead.

"Mommy, what happened? Where am I?"

I was so confused and had no idea where I was or why I was there.

"You're in New York Hospital baby. Don't you remember what happened?"

"I do, but I don't remember everything," I said.

"Well don't go worrying about that now. You just get better."

"Where's Daddy?"

"Your father was here earlier but you were asleep." Her eye contact wandered off and I knew she was lying.

My father never came to see me. He didn't want to see me all fucked up like that.

"How you feeling Chiggy?"

"I'm sleepy Ma. I need some water, my mouth is so dry."

My mother stood up and walked to the table in my tiny hospital room. There was a yellow pitcher of ice water which she poured into a matching small plastic cup. She walked back over to me and gently held my head up enough to take a sip. I was so thirsty that I drank to the point of choking. When I coughed, the knot in my head pulsated heavily as if it was going to explode.

"What happened to my hair Mommy?"

She placed the cup back on the table and grabbed a napkin to wipe the sides of my mouth where the water had dripped.

"Well baby, you got stitches in your head. They had to cut your hair so it wouldn't be all up in the way. But don't worry, the doctors said it will grow back."

I tried to smile but inside my soul hurt. How did my life get to that point? I was still a teenager and there I was lying in the hospital, pistol whipped and unconscious for days.

"Well, when can I go home?"

"Oh, Chiggy, don't think about that right now," my mother said.

I knew her well enough to know when she was trying to keep something from me.

"Ma, when can I go home? What did the doctors say?"

"It's not what the doctors said Chaka. Look, I don't know how to tell you this and I really think it should wait until you get better before I tell you anymore."

"What is it Ma? What?" I slightly raised my voice and could feel my head begin to thump again.

"It's just that, well, when the cops came, they just." Her words were jumbled as she stuttered. "Oh Chaka, why don't you wait until you get a little bit better? I mean you just woke up. You were unconscious for three days. It's just too much for you to handle."

"Ma, tell me. What the fuck is going on?"

I didn't mean to curse but the beating around the bush shit was driving me insane.

"When the police came they found a gun in the kitchen, Chaka. Since your name isn't on the lease or anything, they can't tie that to you but they said the whole thing is drug-related. They found all types of stuff in there. They basically found everything that was in that apartment."

"What does that mean?"

I heard what she was saying but it didn't make sense to me. Drug related? Well of course it was drug related but what did that have to do with my apartment?

"Chaka, in the projects, when an apartment is involved in anything drug related, the Marshalls seize it. Baby, they put a pad lock on the door. You can't go back there anymore."

The words lingered in the air before they finally hit me. Where the hell was I supposed to go? That was my home.

"Well, where are my clothes and my furniture and everything? Did they give you my stuff?"

"Sweetie, everything is gone. When they seize an apartment, they take all the property that's inside of it. There's nothing left." My mother stuck the hook line and sinker deeper into my heart.

Everything I had was gone.

"You know, I spoke to your father and you can always come home."

I turned on my side so that I was facing the wall instead of looking at my mother's face.

"I don't want to talk anymore. I just wanna go to sleep," I snapped.

I knew I had hurt her feelings but I didn't care. The last thing I wanted to do was go home. There was no way I could go back there. Too much had gone on in my life for me to revert into being a little girl again. My mother was right. I should have waited until I had gotten my shit together before I begged her to drop that boulder on me. At least then I would have been better prepared to deal with it.

I closed my eyes and fell asleep while my mother rubbed my back. She kept whispering that everything would be all right. But I knew the truth. My life was never going to be all right again.

CHAPTER 17

"Ms. Adams. Ms. Adams."
The sound of my name being called out, accompanied by my body being jerked, woke me out of my slumber.

"Ms. Adams," the voice said again.

I opened my eyes to find a white man standing over me. His nose protruded immensely from behind his thick bifocals. The white coat and stethoscope instantly identified him as my doctor. He looked sort of young though. Maybe he was an intern or something.

"Ms. Adams, I'm Dr. Rosenberg."

"Great," I thought as he finally identified himself, *"a fucking Jew."*

"How are you feeling today?" He placed the cold stethoscope on my chest and listened.

I took a deep breath and watched as he tinkled with the IVs that were still pumping the liquid into my arm.

"I'm fine." I immediately lost interest in what he was doing once I noticed the other two men behind him.

They didn't look like doctors. Both were white with cocky attitudes that I could sense without them even saying a word. One was short and stocky. His fat cheeks were flushed red as if he was wearing too much blush. Receding from his hairline was an untamed mop of salt and pepper hair. His freckles were scattered about on his face and neck. First impression – he was an old Irish drunk who descended from a long line of cops.

The other guy was the finest white man I had ever seen. Tall, with an athletic physique, his skin was like the olive-colored Italians from all those Mafia movies I watched growing up. His curly hair was jet black as were his hypnotic eyes. He looked good as fuck in a young Andy Garcia type of way. The more I watched him, the more he looked familiar to me. That's when I remembered where I had seen him before. He was the cop inside the car that day I had a fight with Reece. Since then, I somehow managed to continuously bump into him. Whether it was at the store or walking through the blocks late at night, he would just pop up out of the blue. And lo and behold, there he was standing in my hospital room.

"Ms. Adams, these men are detectives with the New York City Police Department," Dr. Rosenberg said. "They want to ask you a few questions. If at any time you don't feel comfortable or if you don't feel well enough to answer them, just let me know."

I knew the doctor didn't really care about how I felt. To him, I was probably just another black face involved in yet another drug related incident.

I didn't say a word. Actually, I had expected it in a way. I just wished they would have at least waited until I got out of the hospital.

The detectives walked closer to my bedside. The first one to start talking was the fat funny looking one with the stereotypical generational prick attitude.

"Yeah, I'm Detective O'Harry and this is my partner Detective Salerno. We want to ask you a few questions."

Just like I thought, he was an Irish prick. I still had no intentions on saying anything to him.

"So what can you tell us?" Detective O'Harry said to me without the least bit of concern for my well-being.

"I don't remember anything."

"Look, you can talk to us here or we can haul your ass off to the station and you can talk there. It's up to you. I could care less one way or the other." His voice was firm.

Perhaps he thought he was intimidating me but obviously he didn't know who the fuck he was dealing with either. His partner stood quietly at the foot of my bed. I matched his gaze and stayed equally mute.

"What were you doing in that apartment?"

"I wasn't. They brought me there."

"They brought you there? Yeah right. So, who are they?" O'Harry obviously didn't believe my response.

"I don't know who brought me there. Perhaps it was the people who did this to me. Why don't you do your job and find them. Then you come back here and YOU tell ME who THEY are."

Salerno interjected in a calm sedated voice. "We want to help you Ms. Adams but we can't do that if you don't help us."

O'Harry shot him a frustrated look. Through his eyes, I could tell I was getting on his nerves. Honestly, the back and forth banter shit was funny to me.

"So, where's Malik?" He stared at me as if he had the upper hand.

His question initially caught me off guard. I wondered where the fuck was he getting his information? How the hell did he know anything about Malik? But instantly, I wiped the shocked look off of my face. I couldn't let O'Harry read me the way I was reading him.

"He's right here, under the bed."

There was no escaping my sarcasm.

He looked at me with pure hatred. His pen and pad were already in his hand waiting to write down everything I said. But I knew the code of the streets. I knew what I had to do. No matter how pissed off I was with Malik, I couldn't snitch on him. Shit, I couldn't even tell them who attacked me.

When you're in the game, you keep your mouth shut and your ears open. I listened to the questions they asked and from that, I surmised that they didn't have anything to tie me to that apartment. My name wasn't on the lease and neither was Malik's. All my mail still went to my mother's house so there was nothing that could identify Chaka Adams as a resident of apartment 6F. As far as the guns and drugs were concerned, I never touched that shit without gloves on. Not even I was that stupid.

I caught Salerno snicker a bit after my comment. He presumed his partner wasn't going to get anywhere with me. By the looks of it, O'Harry was from the old school where they enforced strong arm interrogation tactics. Salerno seemed as if he liked to play it cool. Truthfully, I found him quite intriguing. Although I had never been attracted to a white guy, I'm sure I could have bagged him if I wasn't looking all beat up and whatnot. I liked Salerno but I knew well enough not to trust him. At least not yet anyway.

"Oh, I see, you want to be a smart ass, huh?" O'Harry finally registered a response while his flushed face got redder by the minute.

Salerno came to my rescue as he walked to the other side of my bed where O'Harry was standing. He placed his arm firmly on his partner's shoulder and whispered loud enough for me to hear that I needed some rest and they could try again the next day.

"Yeah," I heckled. "I need some rest. Leave now before I call security on you."

I rolled my eyes and wanted to twist my neck with my words but my body hurt too much for all that. O'Harry stared me down without a blink and I did the same to him. For a second, it felt like we were about to have an old western gun draw. The look of utter disgust was obvious all over his face. I knew he had seen my type before – young, black and just didn't give a fuck. But I also knew that I didn't owe him shit. I didn't owe him an explanation or an answer to any of his stupid ass questions.

"I hope you don't end up in here again or with the way you're going, maybe the next time it will be the morgue," O'Harry said. "We'll be watching you. Trust me, we'll be watching you."

"Yeah, you do that. Matter of fact, why don't you watch your fucking waistline and leave them damn donuts alone." I turned my back toward the wall to purposely let them know they were dismissed.

O'Harry let out a disdainful grunt and walked out of the room. I assumed Salerno accompanied him until I felt a hand touch my back. When I looked over my shoulder, Salerno was there.

"I'm sorry for my partner's behavior," he said.

The sound of his low smooth voice made me forget he was a cop for a second. For some reason, he didn't seem like the ones that I had become accustomed to dealing with.

"Look, Chaka." He caught me by surprise when he used my first name. "You seem like a good girl who got caught up in a bad situation. Between us, we knew who you and Malik were long before this ever happened. Do you really think you could ride around the projects like Prom King and Queen and not catch our attention? I know you don't feel like talking right now so here's my card. If you need to call, for any reason, feel free."

He handed me a small ivory colored business card. **Detective Paul Salerno** was printed on the front along with the New York City Narcotics Task Force symbol. I wanted to rip it up and throw it in his face. But something told me to keep him handy.

Unfortunately, I knew I had already made an enemy out of O'Harry which was the last thing I needed. Sometimes I could kick myself in my own ass for my foul attitude. So, when it came to Salerno, I would force myself to be amiable. It wasn't hard, really. That cop wasn't half as arrogant as his partner and twice as cute. Simply put, it made no sense to burn that bridge.

Salerno quietly let himself out of the small hospital room without saying another word. I looked at his card again and reached over to place it into the nightstand drawer on the side of my bed. As I turned it over, I noticed the handwritten telephone number emblazoned on the back of the card with the words **'personal cell'** next to it.

"Ha," I laughed.

That Salerno guy was slick, I had to give him that much. But I needed to learn exactly what game he was playing before I thought anything more about giving him a call.

I gazed up at the white gravel ceiling with the sounds of machines beeping all around me. Finally, I had an opportunity to be alone and contemplate my next move. From what my mother told me, I no longer had a place to live. I could always go home but of course my pride would have never allowed that.

Playing with the buttons on the side of the bed, I moved up and down until I found a comfortable position. Or at least as comfortable as a hospital bed could be. The clock on the wall read nine o'clock and I watched as the hands slowly clicked around in circles with thoughts of my future wallowing around in my head.

Staying at Ta-Ta's house was an option. Her mother always took us in whenever we needed a place to crash. It wouldn't be like going back home because her moms let us smoke weed and drink right in front of her. But then I remembered her house was full of cousins and aunts along with Zakia and her son. On second thought, Ta-Ta's house was definitely out of the question.

Perhaps Taylor would let me stay with her, I thought. Well, there was really no maybe about that notion. I knew I could live with my cousin for as long as I needed. Regardless of what happened, she would always have my back. Certainly, I would have to start from scratch and work my way back up. But at least, I'd have a roof over my head.

Since I had solved my homeless problem, I tossed and turned until serenity became a welcomed guest. Though sleep felt good, the nightmares of what had become of my life still haunted me. It was impossible for me to find peace even with my eyes wide shut.

CHAPTER 18

By the time both hands on the clock went around in a complete circle, I was awake, packed and ready to go. It was nine in the morning and I was about to be discharged. Almost two weeks of recuperation and I was ready to hit the streets. I wasn't really in a rush, I mean, I didn't have shit to run home to. There was nothing left. No money, no clothes and no Malik. I still hadn't heard a word from him since everything happened. But I couldn't allow myself to think about that and by the way it seemed, he wasn't thinking much about me either.

I sat in the chair with only my hospital gown on and a beige pair of slipper socks that one of the nurses had given me. I didn't know what happened to my clothes but they were probably so full of blood that I was glad to have never seen them again. The bush forming on top of my scalp posed another problem. The stitches still hurt so I really couldn't comb the left side of my head at all. Since my hair was so thick I just did a swoop-around and covered the bald spot. The bandages were still visible despite my attempts but at least I looked half-way presentable or so I thought.

Again, I looked at the clock and wondered who was coming to get me. My mother said she would make sure I had something decent to wear home and a pair of sneakers since I had neither. I should have told her to send me some sunglasses because my left eye was still bloodshot, bruised and swollen.

As soon as I got back to Queensbridge, I planned to go right up to Taylor's house anyway. I couldn't walk around the projects looking all beat the fuck down. Bad enough I was undoubtedly the talk of the gossip hounds but I damn sure wasn't about to give them a visual to accompany their whispers. My image was still everything to me and since I was one of the baddest bitches to hit them streets I had to do everything I could to maintain it.

The door opened and I spun around in my chair. To my surprise, in walked Carmen, Dana and Ta-Ta.

"Hi Mamita! How are you?" Carmen was the first one to speak upon their arrival.

"Hey, y'all finally brought your asses here when I'm about to come home, huh?" I forced a smile through my swollen jaw.

"Oh just shut up and take your clothes." Dana threw a plastic Gap bag on my lap.

When I opened it, I was happy to find all new attire. They bought me a white t-shirt with black nylon jogging pants and a jean baseball cap.

"Girl, your mother told us about your hair and we ain't about to let you walk out of here looking like that," Dana explained as I pulled the cap out of the bag.

She dived on my bed and started to play with the up and down buttons just like a big kid.

"That's right, Mami, so put this on and let's blow this joint." Carmen gently placed it on my head and stuffed the little pieces of my hair up into the cap.

Reaching into her black Gucci bag, she pulled out a compact mirror for me to see for myself.

"Told you." She held the mirror to my face. "You don't even see that, that, how you call it?"

"Bald spot," I inferred, knowing Carmen couldn't find the words to say in English. However, she probably didn't know how to say it in Spanish either.

"Yeah, that bald spot. I wouldn't even know it was there."

"Yo, I need one of these beds in my room." Dana still played with the buttons as her legs went up and down.

Ta-Ta sat quietly by the window staring out at the river. She hadn't said more than two words to me since they arrived. When she first walked in, she gave me a hug but then just avoided me altogether after that.

"Ta-Ta, what's up girl? You all quiet over there and shit," I yelled loud enough to get her attention.

"It's just this hospital thing. I don't like being in hospitals." She paused before finally turning her direction toward me. "Actually, I hope you plan on leaving that nigga alone."

"What?" I was taken aback by her abruptness.

"What you mean what? You heard what I said. I hope you leave that bum ass nigga alone now because he ain't shit."

Carmen felt the need to chime in as well. "You could do much better than him. He's no good, Chaka. Look, where is he at? Huh? Because he sure the hell ain't here."

I couldn't say anything because they were right. There I was on my death bed and Malik hadn't even checked to see if I was still breathing. But then again, I thought maybe something had happened to him. I just needed to talk to him to find out what was going on.

"Look, y'all don't know what's happening right now so just chill the fuck out. I can handle my own business, trust that shit." I stood up and walked to the bathroom to change my clothes.

They were still talking while I got dressed. I heard every word through the cardboard-like bathroom door.

"I don't know what she sees in him anyway," Carmen said.

"Please, that nigga is a bum and you know he's on that dope hard." Ta-Ta was always the loudest and was probably speaking even louder so I could hear everything she had to say.

"Yeah, he fell off," Dana said.

"Fell off? That nigga ain't shit and never was."

Now, these were the same chicks that had their hands out for money from me and my man every chance they got. Yet as soon as things seemed a little bad, they just had to put their say-so in it. And if that wasn't enough, these were the very same bitches that sat up in my house and enjoyed all the luxuries that Malik supplied. Immediately I realized how important it was for me to get out of that hospital and get a hold of Malik. I knew that once I spoke to him, all of the gossip would end and every question would be answered.

As for Ta-Ta saying that he was on dope, I knew that shit was a lie. We never got high on our own supply. This was simply a test of not believing everything I heard. In the hood, people said shit out of pure jealousy. Malik hipped me to that when rumors were going around about him fucking other bitches.

So all the stuff they were talking about in the other room ended up not meaning a thing to me. What did they know anyway? They fucked with nickel and dime small time niggas. I had graduated from that lifestyle back when they were still in training camp.

I quickly pulled the clothes out of the plastic Gap bag, put them on and threw the hospital gown in the garbage. I washed my face softly and looked in the mirror. When I saw my reflection, I wanted to cry. I looked old and worn out. The sensible side was telling me that I was running myself ragged. The stuck-on-stupid side was telling me that I looked like a chick who knew how to get down for hers. My dumb ass didn't know which side to believe.

The conversation ceased once I emerged from the bathroom without the tacky hospital gown I had been sporting for days. That's how you can tell when people are dragging your name through the dirt – they always get quiet when you walk into the room. Just like crickets, they make a lot of noise from afar but when you walk up on them, they get so quiet that you could hear a mouse pissing on cotton.

Ta-Ta passed me a pair of sneakers to throw on my feet. They were an old pair of Hi-Top Reeboks which looked like she ran a marathon in them before giving them to me. She must have been able to tell that I wasn't too thrilled about wearing her hand-me-downs because she immediately got argumentative.

"Look, we ain't have enough money to get you some new ones. So if you don't wanna wear them, I could always take them back."

Ta-Ta's tone was borderline disrespectful but I let it slide. After all, she was doing me a favor and I should have been somewhat appreciative. But damn, I wasn't used to wearing other people's shit. I was the bitch who chicks would borrow clothes from not the other way around. It was at that split second, I was forced to acknowledge that my entire way of living had changed. I went into that hospital one way and I was leaving it as a completely different person.

"You ready girl?" Carmen asked.

"Yeah, let's go." I grabbed my few toiletries and stuffed them into the Gap bag.

"Good, because I need a drink," Dana said.

"Damn girl, it ain't even twelve o'clock. You don't be playing."

I was always amazed at her tolerance for alcohol. That bitch had a liver made of steel.

Everyone laughed except Ta-Ta who solemnly stood up and walked toward the door. I started to think the only reason she came, was to see firsthand how fucked up I really was. I mean, she wasn't comforting at all.

"So what you gonna do now?" Ta-Ta waited until we got to the elevator to finally unleash the shit she had been waiting to say.

It was the sort of question I knew everybody wanted to ask but just didn't have the nerve to do so. They all stayed quiet and turned toward me. I could've killed her for putting me on the spot. Didn't she know that I had already been through enough?

"Look, right now, I just need to get back on my feet and trust me, that won't be a problem," I snapped. "But thanks for asking any motherfucking way."

"Yeah, whatever."

"Whatever, what? Damn, you got a problem with me or something?" I threw my hands up in her face finally fed up with her passive aggressive bullshit.

By that time, the elevator had stopped on our floor and its doors opened. It was full of white people staring out, confused by the homely looking black girls yelling at the top of their lungs. We didn't budge. And by the way we were carrying on, I doubted the people on the crowded elevator wanted us to get on it anyway. I watched the doors close and then reverted my attention right back to Ta-Ta.

"Why don't y'all both just chill out. We in a hospital and y'all acting all ghetto, fighting like y'all enemies and don't even know each other or something." Dana quickly jumped in with every attempt to prevent us from throwing blows.

I glanced over at Carmen, who always had an undercover personal gripe against Ta-Ta and despite normally being the peace keeper, she didn't utter a word. In fact, she wouldn't even look in my direction.

"Yeah, I got a problem. Dana, move, let me tell her a thing or two." Ta-Ta briskly pushed Dana to the side and leaped dead in my face. "Look at you. You let this nigga bring you down. You only eighteen and you in the hospital over a bum ass nigga like Malik. And you still love him, don't you? But where he at? We trying to get money up to get you some clothes and shit and this nigga ain't nowhere around. Where is he Chaka? Dude couldn't even make sure you was aight."

"I don't care Ta-Ta! Whatever happened, happened. You can't knock me for that. If you were my friend, you would UNDER-FUCKING-STAND and not criticize the shit I'm going through right now."

"But that's what I'm saying, I am your friend and I won't sit back and watch you keep making a fool out of yourself for some nigga that don't even give a fuck if you breathing or not. You used to be so pretty but now you looking all tired and shit. You got bruises from this, bruises from that, bruises from anytime Malik feel like beating up on you. Don't think we don't know about him using you for a punching bag because we ain't stupid Chaka."

Once she said that, I knew my secret was blown.

"What goes on in my house is none of your fucking business."

I had to make it seem like things were all right but they saw right through my façade. It's just that I was always taught when you love a man, you can't simply give up because things don't go your way. Neither of them had a man and Ta-Ta had too many men, so what the fuck did they know anyway?

"You know what Chaka," Dana said as she pushed the button for the elevator, "you right. What goes on in your house is your business and not everybody in New York Hospital's business. So why don't y'all settle this shit at home."

That time when the elevator doors opened, we all got on. I stayed away from Ta-Ta because I didn't want to look in her surprisingly judgmental face. The elevator ride was uncomfortably silent but I was too stubborn to say anything to either one of them.

When we got out, the walk down the hospital corridor was eerie without a word muttered between us. I walked ahead of the group because I couldn't stand being in their presence. Someone came up from behind and slid a hand into the back pocket of my pants. I looked and saw that it was Ta-Ta smiling through her teary eyes.

"What do you want?" I turned my head and kept walking.

"Look in your pocket, stupid." She was still trying to act hard despite the sympathetic sound in her voice.

When I reached into my pocket, I pulled out a bag of weed. I couldn't help but laugh and shake my head.

"I figured you would need that after all this bullshit," she said. "See, I do love you, bitch."

I chuckled through my pain. I wasn't happy because I had weed, I was happy because I knew with Ta-Ta, I would always have a friend.

"Chaka, I look up to you. I watch you. You older than me, you know what I'm saying. You should be schooling me and not the other way around."

I stopped walking and looked Ta-Ta dead in her eyes. "Well next time you have something to say to me, please tell me in private and not in the middle of the damn hospital."

She shrugged me off with a fling of her wrist and said, "Bitch, I ain't coming to no more hospitals with your stank ass never again. Now let's go home."

She grabbed my arm and we walked out of the hospital hand in hand. I looked across the river and saw Queensbridge as clear as day. It just went to show me that no matter where I ended up, the projects was never too far away.

"Well damn, is everybody all right now?" Dana asked.

"Yes, because I'm ready to get out of here. Let's catch a cab and go home. I hate hospitals." Carmen stood on the corner trying to flag down a yellow taxi.

I held up the bag of weed for all to see before blurting out, "Hey, why don't we walk some of the way?"

Both Dana and Carmen looked at me and agreed, needing very little persuasion. We all knew what I was walking into once I stepped foot back into the projects. And because they were my friends, they wanted to prolong the agony that faced me for as long as they could.

Instead of catching a cab, we lit a blunt and walked across the 59th Street Bridge back to Queens. Although every step we took was filled with laughter, deep down, we knew that every step was brining me one inch closer to facing my pain.

CHAPTER 19

"**D**id you look in the Daily News?" Taylor yelled into my small bedroom.

I had been living with my cousin since leaving the hospital about two months before. Her son slept in her room and she let me take his. My mother gave me my old bed because Taylor didn't have much furniture. It was either that or lay some blankets down on the cold ass floor. Clearly, I chose my old bed.

The little clothes I managed to accumulate over the past two months were mostly borrowed or shit I had lying around my mother's house. Since there wasn't a dresser or anything, I kept my little belongings in an old duffle bag with the exception of my panties, bras and socks. I didn't have a lot of underwear so they fit perfectly into a cardboard box that I lined with an old pillowcase. It wasn't much but it was all I had.

Taylor never sweated me about rent money. My mother used to give her a few dollars on the low just for letting me stay there. Whenever she went food shopping, she always came upstairs with three or four bags of groceries for Taylor's house too. Both of them knew my pride wouldn't allow me to ask for a handout so whatever deal they had in place, they kept me pretty much out of it.

Word on the street was that Malik would pop up every now

and then, mostly at night, looking all stressed out and grimy. I still hadn't heard from him since everything went down with the Far Rockaway niggas. As bad as I wanted to see him, I had to worry about myself and how I was going to climb out of the hell I was forced to live in.

My mother helped me out when she could but it was nothing like the shit I was used to having with Malik. Instead of Gucci, I was happy to get a few dollars to shop in The Gap. My fly stilettos were replaced with a pair of old sneakers that looked like they were leaning to the side. I couldn't afford to get my nails done like I used to so they were bitten down to little nubs that never grew. The stitches in my head began to heal but since I couldn't afford to get my hair done, I just kept it pulled back into a ponytail covered under a jean baseball cap.

"Did you look in the newspaper?" Taylor asked again from the cracked door of my room.

"No, not today," I said.

She was constantly on me about finding a job. I knew she was steering me in the right direction but who was going to hire a tenth grade drop-out with no skills and no work experience? I kept praying Malik would come to my rescue. After all, I wasn't used to the bum lifestyle, which at that point, was exactly what I was compelled to live.

Because I didn't want to face the stares and finger pointing from the neighborhood bench dwellers, I seldom wandered outside. However, it was the beginning of the summer and I knew I wouldn't be able to hide in the house much longer – especially one without a motherfucking air conditioner.

"Well, I have an interview tomorrow," I lied.

Taylor was in the kitchen about to chef up some breakfast which was something I couldn't do at all. I had absolutely no idea how to cook. My world consisted of take-out, drive-thru and five dollar Fish Fry's which occurred in the hood on a regular basis. Most people said a way to a man's heart was through his stomach. However, my philosophy on the way to his heart had more to do with his dick instead of anything above his waist.

"Yeah, where at?" she asked.

The stove wasn't coming on so I handed her some matches.

She lit the pilot light under the pan and instantly the fire sparked. She cracked three eggs over the melted margarine as the turkey bacon sizzled in the frying pan right next to it. The cheese slowly melted in the pot full of grits that sat on the corner eye with just enough of a flame to keep it warm. We didn't give a fuck that it was almost one o'clock in the afternoon. It was never too late for a hearty hood breakfast.

"Oh, it's just a cashier job at a supermarket," I said.

The food was done and Taylor handed me a plate. I went into my room and watched *Jerry Springer* on the old television I had propped up on a milk crate. Looking around the room, it was a far cry from when Supreme was there. The only remnants of him were the pictures Taylor took when she went upstate on her weekly visits. Thank God, I never had to visit anyone in prison. From what I heard, it was chaotic up there – babies crying and chicks fighting other chicks for visiting their boyfriends. It sounded more like the welfare office instead of a jail.

Taylor was loyal though and went on every visit. I remembered her selling all her furniture and jewelry to pay for his lawyer. She hoped he would beat his case, come home and replace everything she lost. Unfortunately, when he was found guilty and sentenced to ten years, she found herself alone trying to take care of a newborn baby. Bad enough I was struggling to fend for myself, I couldn't imagine trying to do that with a baby to feed.

"So how much are they paying?" Taylor asked.

I had almost forgotten what the hell she was talking about. I made up a quick figure that I thought would be reasonable for a cashier job. I never worked before so I didn't know what to say.

"Um, like seven dollars an hour."

"Oh, that's good money," she replied.

I was shocked. The small amount seemed more like an insult than an income. But when you're living life without a high school diploma or a GED, then I suppose it was the norm.

Thoughts of taking my GED passed my mind from time to time. I wasn't stupid, at least not when it came to them books. I chose to leave high school simply because I didn't want to go, not because I couldn't handle it. The GED programs seemed like they were for dumb ass illiterates who couldn't read and write. Surely, I didn't fit that description so I never bothered to look into taking the test.

"Here Chiggy, take mine too." Taylor handed me her plate when she noticed I was walking toward the kitchen.

"Well if this cashier job doesn't work out, I could always be your maid."

"Funny," she said. "Just make sure you scrape the plate off in the garbage first."

The dishes accumulated in the sink but I was too lazy to wash them. The *itis* was settling in and I was ready to take a nap after that big ass breakfast. Just as I had finally gotten comfortable in my bed, the phone rang.

"Chaka," Taylor called out from her room.

"Who is it?" I knew if it wasn't someone I really wanted to talk to, I wasn't getting out of the bed.

"It's Ta-Ta."

"Could you please bring me the phone?" I whined.

"Now you know I ain't even about to get up."

"Taylor, please. I got cramps."

The sound of her slippers sliding across the floor let me know she fell for it.

"Chaka's House of Beauty is this one of my cuties?" I sang into the phone after Taylor made me promise to click over if another call came through. She was waiting for her daily chat with Supreme.

"You so stupid girl. What you doing boo? You trying to go to The Tunnel tonight?" Ta-Ta was referring to New York City's new "it" club.

"The Tunnel? Come on, you know I don't got no Tunnel money and no Tunnel clothes."

"You think I don't know that? Don't worry about it girl, I got you," she said.

"You got me? Oh, you balling now?"

"Never mind all that. Meet me in front of your building in five minutes so we can go shopping. Bye."

I jumped out of bed with the quickness and threw on the same pair of spandex that I had worn all week. Since I hadn't mustered up enough money to buy any real clothes, the few things I was able to purchase had to get as many wears as possible.

I peeked into Taylor's room and she was already asleep. The *itis* must have gotten to her as well. I locked the apartment door and jetted down the stairs to Ta-Ta who was sitting in a cab in front of my building. She already had a blunt lit for our ride to Steinway Street. The cab driver didn't mind if we smoked or rather, we never asked for permission.

I couldn't wait to find out where she was getting all her money from so I just blurted out my questions. "What the fuck is up and how the fuck you got all this money?"

She explained that she had met some Spanish dude from Washington Heights who, by my assumption, was holding some serious paper. He was meeting us at The Tunnel that night with a bunch of his friends. She didn't say if she was fucking him or not but if he was breaking her off with money, she had to be giving up some pussy. Immediately, I started scheming in my head. If she was able to trick on papi like she was doing, I was definitely going at one of his friends.

We shopped for about two hours going in and out of practically every store on the five block strip. I got some tight Guess jeans and a cute little black off the shoulder top from Express. Ta-Ta even sprung for a pair of black sandals from a new shoe store that had just opened up. It seemed like an eternity since I had been shopping. I felt like Julia Roberts in that scene from *Pretty Woman.*

I looked down at my nails and wondered what I was going to do with them. No amount of nail polish could help the way they were looking. Before I could say anything, Ta-Ta was already leading me toward the nail salon to get some acrylic tips. Since she was paying, I made sure to get the most expensive design on every finger and toe. Once we were done with our nails, we stopped at the Dominicans and got a fresh wash and set. Finally, I felt like my old self again.

As soon as we got back to the hood, I rushed upstairs to shower and put on my new clothes. I felt like a kid on the first day of school – eager to pop tags and come outside fresh to death.

"Wow, Chiggy, you look so cute." Taylor did a double take as I emerged from my bedroom dressed to the nines.

I took the pins out of my hair and let my doobie fall down my back. Luckily I still had some left after the Dominicans chopped off all the dead ends. When I looked in the mirror, I noticed how skinny I had gotten due to all the stress. In my opinion, I still looked good but in reality, I looked like a bag of bones.

"Can I use some of your eyeliner?" I had already pulled the pencil out of her makeup bag and started putting some on before I asked.

"And you're wearing makeup? Let me find out you got a date or something."

Truthfully speaking, I needed the makeup to cover the dark circles under my eyes and the black marks I had accumulated from the many blows my face encountered.

"Well, have fun and don't forget about your interview tomorrow," she said.

I pretended not to hear her and asked to borrow her MAC lip gloss which she wore religiously. She surprised me by parting with it but it was just the thing I needed to complete my look.

After one last glance in the mirror, I was ready to go. I gave Taylor a kiss on her cheek as her eyes welled up at the sight of me feeling good about myself again. The way she was carrying on, you'd think I was heading out to the prom or something.

Ta-Ta told me to meet her at her house which meant I would have to walk across the projects to get to her block. I didn't care because I was looking cute and wanted everybody to see me. They had all thought I would have fallen off but that night, I felt like I was back on top.

As I pranced past the bench dwellers who were seated in their usual spots in front of my building, I heard all the whispering as soon as they thought I was out of reach of their voices. Sure they smiled and told me how cute I looked but as soon as I had my back turned, they started with the project gossip.

"Oh she must got herself a new man."

"That's her problem, she always thinking she cute."

"She painted those pants on because they are way too tight. Her little hot ass is gonna get a yeast infection."

Hood gossip was never-ending whether you were up or down. Actually, it was the same gossip that kept me on my toes. As long as people were talking about me, I must have been doing something right. If I wasn't on their minds, my name surely wouldn't have been spouting from their mouths. Their gossip only meant one thing to me and that was, simply put, they were still thinking about me.

I had almost made it to Ta-Ta's block before a familiar voice stopped me dead in my tracks. There was no need to turn around. I could tell once he called out my name, it was Malik. As I watched him approach, so many feelings ran through my body. The logical part of me was mad enough to attack him but the emotional part was just happy that he was standing there in front of me.

"Hey Chako."

It felt as though I hadn't heard him say my name in years. Words couldn't come out of my mouth while I stood there shocked to be face to face with him. I had been preparing for that conversation ever since everything happened but at that moment, I couldn't remember a single word.

"Chako, you look good baby."

"Malik?"

Finally, I said his name unsure if it was really him or just a figment of my imagination.

"Yeah, it's me. What? I can't get a hug?"

Once he grabbed me in his arms, our surroundings disappeared. I didn't hear the cars passing by or the loud music coming from the apartment window above us. The constant hustle of the projects came to a screeching halt. Malik, at that second, was the only thing that mattered to me.

I lavished in his embrace for what felt like an eon. The tears fell from my eyes, surely messing up the mascara I was wearing. His heart beat furiously next to mine. He felt the same but smelled different. Perhaps it was his stench that brought me back to reality.

"What are you doing out here?" I finally managed to pull myself out of his trance.

"I had to come out here to see somebody." His lips nervously twitched as he spoke.

"You couldn't call me or nothing? How could you do that to me?" I was pleading for an answer that I felt I rightfully deserved.

His eyes stared blankly into mine. Two months had changed him to where he was almost unrecognizable. His weight had plummeted drastically down to about 130-pounds soaking wet. The goatee he used to keep shaped up looked patchy and in desperate need of a comb. Both of his hands were so ashy, they appeared as if he was playing in flour all day. Despite his clothes being about three sizes too big for his slender body, they were so dirty that they could practically stand up on their own. People told me he was looking bad but I didn't expect to see it up close and personal.

"Chak, I know what happened was fucked up but I did it for you."

"For me? You can't be serious."

"Nah, for real. Come on now Chaka. I didn't want those punk ass niggas to know we was still together. I didn't want you to get involved."

He didn't want to get me involved? He should have thought about that before I was hit with a pistol and laid up in a hospital.

"Anyway," he continued, "you don't gotta worry about them no more. I took care of it. They won't be around here ever again. We good now."

I heard what he said and knew it could have only meant one thing – they were dead. He didn't have to say it verbatim but I knew the only way he would've stopped that hit was by making sure they never breathed again. Clearly the drugs hadn't impacted his ability to go rogue. That nigga was still a beast whether he was strung out or not. But in the streets, some things were just better left unsaid so I took heed and moved on to the next topic.

"So Chaka," Malik ran his hand through my hair, "that's why I couldn't come and check on you. I ain't wanna bring that bullshit around you anymore baby."

His words felt comforting and for a second, as I looked into his eyes, I remembered the old Malik. Memories of our old life with the money, the apartment and the notoriety flooded my brain. Somehow, he still had that power over me.

Sensing I wouldn't be able to confront him the way I had rehearsed time and time again, I pulled away and told him I had to go meet Ta-Ta.

"You got a number so I can call you?"

"I'm staying at Taylor's house. You remember her number right?"

"Yeah, but let me write it down. You know I be forgetting shit on the regular." He scrambled around looking for a piece of paper, continuously searching every pocket of his dingy army fatigues.

As the seconds went by, I grew more annoyed that I was even in his presence. I reached into the black Coach bag that Taylor lent me and handed him a receipt.

"Here, use the back of this."

"Nah, Chak, it ain't that. I just lost a hundred dollars. And damn, all my money is at my mother's crib."

"Oh well, maybe you'll find it later. But anyway, I gotta go meet Ta-Ta." I was trying to get away from him as quickly as possible.

"Wait Chak, let me hold twenty dollars baby. You know I got you."

I couldn't believe he was asking me for money. In the past, my hands were always out to him and there he was begging to hold something. I reached into my borrowed purse once again and handed him a twenty. I only had forty dollars to my name but I knew Ta-Ta had cash so I wasn't sweating it. Besides, I used to tip my hair dresser twenty dollars in my former life so parting with that chump change wasn't going to kill me.

"Good looking out Chak, you know I got you. We gonna be all right, young love. Watch, I'ma get shit right with us."

As he tried to kiss me, I hurried to turn my face forcing his chapped lips to land on my cheek instead. There was no telling where his mouth had been and with the looks of him, it could've been anywhere.

"Oh, I can't kiss you now?" He had the audacity to sound offended.

"No, you can't. And you lucky I even gave you twenty dollars. I'll see you later Malik."

Finally I turned to leave and thought he'd have something to say in response to his obvious dismissal. However, by the time I turned back around, he was half-way down the block.

Funny thing was, he never even wrote my number down.

CHAPTER 20

Walking to Ta-Ta's block had given me some time to shake off the remnants of seeing Malik. I couldn't believe he allowed himself to fall off so badly. Never in a million years would I have imagined he'd be so down and out. Then again, I never thought I would be either.

Bumping into him left me with an uneasy feeling. There were a million things I wanted to say but from the looks of it, I knew the rumors were true. Malik wasn't the same man I had known and talking to him wouldn't put the pieces of my life back together. Instead, I had to force myself to move on to the next opportunity, which at that point, lied with Ta-Ta and her new connects.

I spotted her standing on the hill outside of the bodega.

"Hollywood," I yelled from across the street.

I started calling Ta-Ta by that name once she began taking pages out of Lil' Kim's wardrobe book. That day was no exception. She was wearing pink leather hottie shorts that outlined her pussy lips giving them the perfect upside down triangle look. The leather matching vest was unbuttoned just enough so even Stevie Wonder could see her plump double-D cleavage. Pink highlights poked out of the long slicked down weave ponytail she was sporting. Even in my new clothes, I felt small in comparison to her larger-than-life persona.

It was only eight o'clock which was entirely too early to step out to a club in the city so we decided to head to the neighborhood bar for a drink. Even when the sun was out, the bar was always full of people looking for a party without stepping out of their comfort zones.

The spot, which we all referred to as The Pub, was a block away from the projects but it might as well have been right in the heart of the hood. If you came to Queensbridge and were old enough to drink or at least looked like you were, you had to make at least one visit to The Pub. It was no bigger than my small project apartment and stayed dimly lit but it was still a national landmark, at least that's the way we saw it.

Pictures of Queensbridge's quasi-celebrities adorned the walls reflecting the many dreams deferred from the talented ghosts of the past. There were black and white pictures of Tony, the semi-professional boxer from Tenth Street and Candy, the chick from Vernon Boulevard who thought she was a supermodel after only appearing in one video. She was a background dancer nonetheless.

Of course there were pictures of all the Queensbridge rappers, Nas, Mobb Deep, MC Shan, Marley Marl and Roxanne Shanté. They were, after all, considered Queensbridge royalty and we celebrated them every chance we could. We even repped for little Ron Ron, who hadn't even finished high school yet. Somehow we all knew that doofy ass nigga was making it to the NBA so his spot on the wall was front and center as well.

But what gave The Pub its true hometown appeal were the pictures of all the Queensbridge old timers. I laughed every time I looked at the one of my mother with her afro and platform shoes. One of my missions in life was to get my picture up on the wall right beside hers. Even then, I knew somehow, I'd have my spot in Queensbridge history.

As usual, The Pub was crowded when we got there. Since there weren't any open stools or tables, we crammed our way to a spot at the bar and ordered our drinks.

"Let me get a vodka and cranberry," Ta-Ta yelled to the Dominican bartender. "And give Chaka a Hennessey and Pepsi."

She pulled a wad of bills from out of her pink Fendi clutch. I peeped her roll of money but didn't say anything. It was too crowded and loud at the bar to get into all of that. However, I made a mental note to inquire more about her come-up later on that night.

The DJ was blasting *"Before I Let Go"* by Frankie Beverly and Maze which packed the small dance floor with people who were too young to really remember that song. Still, they were dancing and belting out every lyric at the top of their lungs.

"Come with me to the bathroom," Ta-Ta whispered into my ear. "I need to tell you something."

I obliged and grabbed her hand making our way through the crowd. All eyes were on us and I loved every minute of it. Bitches hated us because we were still young and managed to look better than the typical project chicks on their best days.

As we shoved and pushed our way through the huddles of people, I felt somebody slap me on my ass. Assuming it was just an accidental bump, I really didn't pay it any attention at first. It wasn't until I felt the second and much harder slap that I was ready to flip and smack the shit out of the person doing it. However, once I turned around, I couldn't believe who it was.

"Jamere?" I squealed out of both shock and delight.

"What's up baby girl?" He grabbed me up into a bear hug.

"Oh my God, what are you doing here?"

I vividly remembered the last visual I had of him standing naked in my bathroom.

"I just got in town and these clowns dragged me down here for a drink."

When he pointed toward his table, I saw all of the Enforcers surrounded by bottles upon bottles of Moët. Undoubtedly, I had chosen the perfect night to be all dressed up and looking pretty. Surely, they could appreciate the fact that I still hadn't fallen off despite what happened with Malik.

Ta-Ta tugged at my hand pulling me toward the bathroom. I made Jamere promise to stay put until I got back. There was no way in hell I was letting him leave without an opportunity for us to catch up.

The bathroom only had one toilet so it always raised

suspicion when two girls went in at the same time. But everybody was already too drunk by then to notice. Once inside, Ta-Ta locked the door behind us and proceeded to pull a folded dollar bill from her bra.

"What you gotta tell me that's so important?" I asked while checking my makeup out in the mirror above the sink.

"Yo, you gotta try this shit." She gently unfolded a twenty dollar bill lined with cocaine that sparkled down the crease as the light reflected off of it.

"What? Where'd you get that from?"

I had heard about all the cokehead cutie pies roaming the hood but up until then, I had never tried it myself.

"Them niggas from uptown got me loving this shit. Let me show you how to do it."

Ta-Ta folded a matchbook cover into a perfect angle and I watched as she scooped a small amount of cocaine onto the corner of it. She placed the bill on the edge of the sink freeing her hand to hold down her left nostril. As she put the matchbook into her nose, she took a long sniff and her eyes opened wide.

"Damn, this shit is raw," she said before dipping the matchbook back into the massive pile of cocaine and scooping up a little more.

She then switched nostrils and took another sniff. The coke disappeared into her nose which seemed to open wider with every inhale.

"Here, you try it." She handed the bill and matchbook cover to me as I looked down at it both confused and curious at the same damn time.

"How does this shit make you feel?" I wondered aloud while trying to mimic everything she had just taught me.

When I sniffed the cocaine I felt it burn as it softly traveled up my nasal passage. One single tear fell from my eye as I felt a rush I had never felt before. I didn't know if I was taking too much or too little but what I did know was that the shit felt good so I just kept scooping and sniffing.

"Chaka, chill out," Ta-Ta warned on my fifth or sixth bump. "You supposed to only take one hit in each nostril. Damn, you acting like a hoover."

I giggled, the effects of the cocaine already taking its toll. Carefully I folded the bill back up and handed it to her. We both checked the mirror to make sure we didn't have any powder on our noses before making our way out of the bathroom.

As I emerged, everything seemed much more alive. My steps had more sex appeal and my eyes darted around with keen precision. The cocaine made me feel invincible. I surveyed the scene of The Pub and even the black and white pictures popped with color. The wood paneling on the walls shined as though they had a fresh coat of varnish. My heart pounded heavily along with the grinding beat of Vanity's *"Nasty Girl"* pumping from the speakers which seemed to have gotten ten decibels louder.

"Now I'm saying, can I get a drink," I yelled to Jamere as I sashayed to where he was still sitting with the other Enforcers.

Ta-Ta disappeared into the crowd and if she felt anything like me, she was somewhere dancing or talking somebody's ear off. My facial expression couldn't mask my high. Trying to look as serious as possible only caused me to be more conscious of not looking high which probably made me look higher. I know, the shit made no sense to me either. But then again, I was so blasted, that making sense was the furthest thing from my mind.

My thoughts were racing and I found it hard to pay attention to any one thing. Although very little words came out of my mouth, it was difficult to stop my lips from constantly moving. I silently prayed to myself that Jamere wouldn't notice.

"Look at you getting all fat." I teased Jamere while taking a sip of my drink. It was like I was drinking water because the cocaine had numbed every taste bud in my mouth.

"Yeah, it's that down south food," he said.

"Nah, you getting some loving from one of them big booty, fish and grits eating girls down there."

"Come on Chaka, ain't nobody down there. I'm still waiting for you." His response confused me because I couldn't tell if he was joking or being serious.

Since the cocaine had me feeling bolder than usual, I reached under the table and grabbed his dick. "Let me see if everything got fatter while you been gone."

"You can't handle that." He quickly moved my hand away from his bulge. "But I'm happy to see you're all right now."

I knew that conversation was going to happen eventually. And as expected as it was, I had no intentions on discussing it. I was high and trying to have fun. The drug made me numb to the pain I had endured.

After that first bump, I instantly knew cocaine would always be my crutch.

"Yeah, I'm all right. It ain't nothing. But your man is a bitch though."

"I told you to watch him Chaka."

"I know but I ain't think he would get down like that."

I explained to Jamere that I had just bumped into Malik and continued blabbing about his appearance. Unlike me, Jamere had known Malik was on that shit for a while. In fact, everyone knew. Clearly, I was the last person to realize it. I guess the closest ones are always the furthest from the truth.

"So, you staying with me tonight?" His question left me completely dumbfounded.

"What? You better stop playing."

"I'm serious. Here, I'm staying at the Crowne Plaza by La'Guardia Airport." He nonchalantly slid me his room key across the table.

Though I was turned on by his aggressive stance, I declined the invitation.

"Whatever, I won't be coming to your damn room. We don't get down like that punk."

Looking over my shoulder, I saw Ta-Ta talking to Dana who had snuck into the bar without me noticing. The conversation with Jamere was slowly killing my buzz especially since I was trying my hardest to seem like I didn't have a buzz at all. The cocaine made it grueling for me to sit in one place let alone hide the effect it had over me.

"Well I'm gonna go over there and say hi to Dana. I'll see you before I leave." I got up from the table and walked to where my friends were perched against the bar.

I could tell by Dana's wide eyes, which were usually chinky, that she had made a pit stop into the bathroom too. It made me wonder why I was the last person on the face of the Earth to try cocaine.

"And where y'all think y'all going?" Dana shouted.

We should have invited her to The Tunnel as well but Ta-Ta had her own agenda. Unfortunately for Dana, it only included me. I didn't complain because I was in no mood to fight for attention once we got with the Spanish dudes.

I whispered for Ta-Ta to pass me the bill so I could go back to the bathroom for another hit. I could barely feel the effects of the three drinks I gulped down but the cocaine feeling was something I didn't want to lose.

When I got into the bathroom and opened the bill, I was hyped to find that Ta-Ta had added even more powder. I could rock all night if I wanted. Cocaine was by far the best high I had ever experienced. Throughout my years, I've tried everything from weed, mescaline tabs, acid and even mushrooms, but there was nothing like the rush I got from a sniff of blow.

After taking a few hits in each nostril just as Ta-Ta had shown me, I checked my nose in the mirror and stepped out of the bathroom feeling rejuvenated. I saw Jamere watching my every move so I smiled at him but was not about to go back to his table. Pretending not to be high was actually fucking up my high and that seemed very counter-productive.

"Paco, put my drink in a plastic cup to go," Ta-Ta yelled to the bartender. "Come on Chaka, we out."

Dana was too deep into her own cocaine induced conversation to notice we were leaving but I still gave her a hug goodbye before slipping out of the bar without saying anything to Jamere.

We walked to the corner and caught a yellow cab into the city. My night had officially begun. Between the rush of the cocaine and the possibility of meeting a nigga with some money, there was no stopping me. My comeback was going to be epic even if I had no idea where that road would lead. Clearly, I was oblivious to the dead end I would eventually ride into. But life was all about the ride, wasn't it? And I was determined to buckle up and ride that motherfucker until the wheels fell off.

CHAPTER 21

"**S**o, how did you get all this coke?" I asked Ta-Ta before the cab driver had an opportunity to turn the meter on.

She took a sniff from the bill. "Girl, its them Puerto Rican niggas I was telling you about. Remember when I told you I was going down south for the weekend?"

I vaguely recalled her mentioning something about leaving but I was too wrapped up in trying to keep a roof over my head to give it much thought. "Yeah, you went to see your grandmother or somebody, right?"

"Well, that's what I said but I really went down there to bring some bricks to one of this nigga's connects in North Carolina."

"You did what? Ta-Ta you crazy. You took the bus all the way down south to bring somebody some drugs? What if you woulda got caught, stupid?"

"How I'ma get caught? Greyhound don't check your bags. So anyway, peep this, that nigga gave me five thousand dollars just for making the trip."

My eyes widened and my head cocked to the side before I shouted, "Five thousand dollars?"

The sight of that much money danced around in my brain. Since the night of the Far Rockaway attack, I hadn't seen a fraction of that type of cash. If I played my cards right and got in good with those dudes, there was no doubt in my mind that I could rebuild my life to where it once was.

"Yup and Chaka I'm telling you, they got money. And I mean, real money. All these niggas in Queensbridge know them."

"How they know them?"

"What? These ain't no small time niggas." Her abrupt response almost sounded as if she was offended. "People from the hood go uptown and buy bricks from them. You think these penny and nickel motherfuckers out here is doing something? They ain't shit compared to papa. That's my word."

"Damn, you fucking with the drug dealer's drug dealer!"

Dollar figures immediately began to ca-ching like a cash register in my brain. She didn't have to say another word. I was completely amped up about meeting the Puerto Ricans or whatever the fuck they were. Suddenly, I couldn't wait to get to The Tunnel.

As we drove through the streets of Manhattan, I became hypnotized by the bright lights of the city and its ample opportunities for action. Our cab pulled up to the red light on the corner of Eighteenth Street and Seventh Avenue. While waiting for it to change, a white Mercedes Benz pulled up right next to us. The windows were tinted black like a limousine's and the rims kept spinning even while the car was motionless. As I watched in awe, I saw the same Benz pull up next to it except it was silver with 20-inch wheels that sparkled. Then, like some Secret Service type shit, another Benz pulled up beside us. It was black with the same tinted windows and shiny rims.

"Yo, that's them right fucking there," Ta-Ta said when she noticed the cars.

I thought she was joking until she reached over me and began to roll down the old-fashioned window handle on the taxi door. Her big breasts practically smothered me as she leaned over to yell out of the window.

"Yo," she shouted.

Either it was the music in their cars or the fact that we were at a crowded Manhattan intersection, but nobody budged.

"YOOOOO!!" That time she started waving her hands out of the car along with her shout out.

It must have worked because the window of the white Benz rolled down just enough to see the driver motion for us to get into the car with him. Ta-Ta pulled some money out of her bag and shoved it through the tiny slot of the bulletproof window that separated us from the cabbie. Then, we made a dash to the Benz right in the middle of the street. Horns were honking, people were yelling out of their windows – it was chaos but the Puerto Ricans just sat there holding up traffic and not giving a fuck about it. From the looks of it, we held cars up for nearly a block but not one person had the heart to walk up and complain about it. Those motherfuckers owned the night and they knew it.

I jumped into the back seat while Ta-Ta got into the front. The first thing I noticed was the car's butter soft tan leather interior. It felt softer than my borrowed Coach bag. Before then, I had thought Malik's Camry was a luxury car.

Don't blame me. I had barely gone outside of my six block radius to know the difference.

Ta-Ta started talking to the driver who I caught looking back at me through his rearview mirror. From what I could see, he looked good as fuck. His seat was reclined far back enough to get a good look of his profile. The arm he had placed on the steering wheel was flooded with an iced out bracelet. I had never seen so many diamonds on one piece of jewelry. The gold was dark and heavy, unlike that cheap shit from The Colosseum on Jamaica Avenue. On his other arm, which was leaning on the driver's console between him and Ta-Ta, he rocked the same Rolex watch worn by Biggie Smalls in one of his videos. If Biggie had it on, I knew that shit was expensive. Immediately, I was hooked. Whoever he was, he was somebody that could take me to the next level. If there was ever a time for me to choose up, that time came the moment I stepped foot into that car.

He pulled into the parking lot across the street from the club quickly followed by the other two cars. From the corner of my eye, I noticed him hand the valet guy a couple of hundred dollar bills for the three cars and then walk away from his change without giving it a second thought.

Yup, shorty was on some real Boss type shit.

Ta-Ta briefly introduced me to the guys as we approached the red velvet ropes to get into the club. I couldn't remember all their names but they all sounded like Juan, Jose, or Enrique. I just smiled and waved at each still unsure as to who would be my sponsor for the night. I remembered who the Boss was and that's all that really mattered. His name was Manuel or Manny as I was told to call him. He said something to his friends in Spanish and I wished I would have paid more attention in school so I'd know what the fuck he was saying.

As soon as the bouncers saw Manny step out from the crowd, they immediately pulled back the ropes and we walked right in bypassing the metal detectors and ID check. He didn't have to say a word, his presence alone was just enough.

As we walked by the crowd of people begging to get into the club, I could hear whispers. I giggled when I heard one girl say to another, *"Oh, those bitches scored for the night."*

My ears were ringing with a surge of notoriety when a guy forewarned his friend, *"Nah, let them niggas go ahead. That's that nigga right there."*

My esteem grew with every confirmation thus further proving to myself that I, in no way, was born to be mediocre. My spot with the shot-callers was solidified by walking into The Tunnel with Ta-Ta's people.

We were personally guided to a secluded VIP section by the club's owner. The table was set with bottles of Moët, Belvedere and Hennessey which were sitting in silver buckets atop mounds of ice. By the time we sat down, a cute little Dominican-looking waitress was already pouring our drinks. Manny and Ta-Ta whispered among themselves while his homeboys were taking shots and pulling chicks over to our area. Since I still had the bill with the cocaine in it, I walked off and made my way to the bathroom. It didn't make any sense for me to play the third wheel when Manny nor his friends seemed the least bit interested. My ego was shot. I looked good, maybe a little worn out from the bullshit I was going through but in my eyes, I was still a trophy chick. So for the life of me, I couldn't understand why I wasn't getting any play. Hopefully the nose candy I was about to ingest would help me feel like myself again.

Once I came out of the unisex bathroom, I was glad to see Ta-Ta. She had finally pulled herself away from Manny, who was in deep conversation with the waitress at that point. I put on my best catwalk and glided across the packed dance floor.

"Where you slid off to?" Ta-Ta asked.

"Girl, whatever, you all boo'd up with Rico Suave over there."

I hoped a little attitude would mask my jealousy.

"Boo'd up? Oh hell no! I'm trying to get this nigga to break us off."

"Break us off how?"

"Girl, you know what we could do if we had our own connect? Shit, all these niggas go uptown to cop. We could bring that shit right there to them. What other bitches you know got bricks in the hood? We could kill it."

I could tell Ta-Ta was serious from the look in her eyes. I had been around drugs enough to understand the game. But I was never a drug dealer on my own. Part of me knew I wasn't built for that but another part, the greedy part, couldn't walk away from the possibility of seeing all that money. This would be the only opportunity I'd have to get that lifestyle back. The life I knew, where I never had a need or a want, could be mine again if we made the right moves.

"So anyway, you need to be a little nicer and throw that nigga a smile or something," Ta-Ta quipped.

When we got back to our table, Manny's friends had scooped up some groupies who seemed to be ecstatic to have been invited into VIP. I guess even then, it didn't take much to impress a basic bitch.

Manny wasn't fazed by the onslaught of pussy vying for his attention. He sat there alone and quietly observed the crowd. I took note of how he carried himself. He was reserved and laid back which was so atypical of all the drug dealers I'd been around. While most dudes I knew from the projects were the loud, wild-out types, Manny was the complete opposite. However, he didn't come off as a punk even without the need to flaunt his power. I liked his style immediately.

I made my way to where Manny was sitting and poured a drink. He wasn't too approachable but he really didn't scare me off either. Although he didn't seem like the small-talk type of guy, I figured I'd give it a try anyway. After all, I was known for my gift of gab so I knew once I got to talking to him, we'd hit it off.

"So, why are you here sitting all by yourself?" I asked.

"Waiting on you Mamita."

With his thick Spanish accent, he could have easily been plucked from a scene straight out of *Scarface*.

"Well here I am. But I mean, really, you got all these girls here and you ain't paying them any attention. Why is that?"

He gave the room a once-over and turned back to face me. "I think I got the one I want right here."

He knew all the right words to say. I couldn't help but blush like a school girl with a crush. Since the ice was finally broken between us, it was much easier to get him to loosen up so that I could work my way into his head. I found out that he was from Columbia originally but moved to New York when he was a kid. His family had some political ties in his country or something like that but he didn't go into too much detail which was a good thing. The less I knew the better. He wasn't a dumb nigga either. He grew up in the posh Croton-on-the-Hudson suburb and went to New York's elite private schools. He definitely came from money. Once he got older, one thing led to another and he found himself continuing his family's business by becoming one of the major cocaine suppliers in the city. If I hadn't fully realized who he was before, I quickly found out after that conversation. I'd describe him as a thug with a sophisticated swagger and believe me that shit said a lot.

Manny seemed impressed with my level of intellect as well. Though I perpetuated the hood mentality, in all reality, I was a bookworm who got free and a little too loose. I was always smarter than the average chick but I learned how to dumb myself down in order to fit in. However, when I met Manny, I turned the "white girl" on instantly. And when I was on, I was turned all the way up.

Before we realized it, it was already three o'clock in the morning and definitely time to leave. Lames were the only people who stayed in the club long enough for the lights to come on. I looked over the dance floor and noticed Ta-Ta had finally made her way back to the VIP section. She had been floating through the crowd high on coke and buzzing off the liquor all night.

"Well Mamita, I'm gonna see you again," Manny said as he stood to exit.

I was taken aback by his sudden dismissal. At the very least, I was expecting him to try to jump off for the night.

"How you gonna see me again if you don't even have my number?"

I was hoping my response was enough to flirt my way to an invite into his bed. Instead, he whistled loud enough for Ta-Ta to hear him. She walked over and he whispered in her ear. Whatever he was saying must have been what we needed to hear because her eyes lit up like a Christmas tree. I was trying to be nosy but it was useless. The music was pumping too loud for me to hear a peep from either of them.

As if on cue, his boys started making their way toward the side exit door once Manny and Ta-Ta had finished talking. He looked at me and motioned a hand salute and a coy wink of the eye. I felt cheated out of a hug but I supposed it was good enough that he even acknowledged me.

"Girl, I don't know what you did but we in there," Ta-Ta said once Manny was out the door.

"What? What are you talking about?"

I was completely confused. I thought since he wasn't trying to fuck me that he really didn't find any use for me.

"Yo, he just said he's gonna fuck with us! We 'bout to kill the hood!"

In an instant, my world had changed. By getting with Manny, we would be at the top of the Queensbridge drug game. I had never seen money like that before and I knew for damn sure that Ta-Ta hadn't either. But as quickly as my excitement grew, so did my nerves. I didn't know shit about selling serious weight. I might have slung a rock or two when I needed a quick couple of bucks but Ta-Ta was talking about some real *Paid in Full – Money Making Mitch* type of shit and I wasn't sure if I was ready for all that.

She must have noticed my hesitation because she was quick to jump in with some reassurance.

"Don't worry Chaka. We got this. We get the shit from him, we hit them niggas off in the hood, we pay Manny back and we keep the rest. It's that simple. I'm telling you, this shit is about to pop off. Thelma and Louise style fa' real." She held her hand up for a high five.

I left her hanging and shook my head in disbelief that I was about to blindly jump into the craziest shit I had ever done in my life.

"Yeah, Thelma and Louise style. But just remember, both of them bitches died at the end."

Ta-Ta laughed but somehow I could tell she knew I wasn't joking. We had a lot to lose if her plan didn't work. Unfortunately for us, we would soon find out just how much was really at stake.

CHAPTER 22

Word quickly got around the hood that we had the connect. Within a couple of months, we were moving more cocaine in a day than the average project dealer could even imagine. Manny was impressed with the quick turn-around and started giving it to us cheaper which meant our profit increased significantly

Since there were three other projects within walking distance from Queensbridge, we pretty much supplied the whole Long Island City area. Niggas didn't have to take a cab ride and risk getting robbed or pulled over by the police when they could just cop from us. We were smart about it though. Only the big bosses knew we were holding since they were the money-makers anyway. They bought weight, stepped on it a few times then sold it to the nickel and dime hand-to-hand young bucks standing on the corner.

Every now and then, we'd switch up our routine so there was little to no chance of predicting our next move. We both grew up in Queensbridge so nobody was going to try to hurt us or get at us. Shit, the hood practically protected us. There was no way somebody was coming into those six blocks to fuck with us and expect to make it out alive.

We had stash spots spread throughout all ninety-six buildings. They were real incognito and far from conventional.

We didn't fuck with crackheads, hoodrats or family members. Instead, we had the drugs hidden in people's apartments who went to church every week, worked all day, barely came outside and hardly ever intermingled with the locals. I was amazed at the lengths in which people would go for a couple of stacks every month. From preachers, nursery school teachers and grandmothers, it was surprising just what a person would risk if the price was right.

As our clientele grew, so did our money. Tata's aunt moved down south and she let us take over her two-bedroom apartment. Once we had our own spot, we really felt like we were making moves. Our closets were packed with the latest shit from Gucci to Versace. Manny showed us all the spots in Manhattan that had the best clothes. We perused the racks at Bloomingdales, Bergdorf Goodman and Saks Fifth Avenue. I couldn't believe that I lived in New York my whole life and had never shopped anywhere but Steinway Street.

In true fashion, the project groupies jumped right back on my shit. The funny looks I got when I was down and out had been replaced with requests to borrow clothes, bags, shoes and money. Dudes were intimidated even more once they realized my money was coming from my own hustle and not the next nigga's pockets.

I had heard the saying that money can't buy happiness. But the truth of the matter was that it did. Who can smile when you have to worry about where your next dollar is going to come from or how you will be able to put food on the table? Fuck that, I had struggled long enough and I was determined to never go back to that life ever again.

My climb up the ladder would later be overshadowed by my plummet, but for the time being, the air smelled so much better at the top – *breath in, breath out.*

CHAPTER 23

The day started off fine. I was meeting my mother for our weekly hair appointment and then we were going to brunch at Bel-Aire Diner. Ta-Ta was on her way uptown to pick up from Manny because we were completely out of product and the first of the month was right around the corner. We had a dude coming to cop so we already knew the cash was about to flow. After business was handled, we had planned to meet up with Dana and Carmen for a Girls' Night Out in the city.

I woke up and called my mother to make sure she was getting ready.

"Hello." My dad's voice came through the phone after it rang a few times.

"Hi Daddy, what's up?"

"Hey Chiggy. Nothing much. Just sitting here hungry because my wife didn't cook any breakfast. She claims to be going out to eat with my daughter who didn't think about inviting her hungry father along."

"Daddy," I whined, "it's a girl's day."

"What? I get manicures too. I'm smooth like that."

I was happy that my father and I had reconciled. It took a while for us to get beyond the big fight but eventually a brief hello turned into a quick laugh or joke and before long, we were sitting back on the couch watching movies together.

Unlike most of the chicks I grew up with, I had a father at home. Sadly, I can count on one hand how many of my friends were raised the same way. Yet people wonder why Black women, especially those of us from the ghetto, have such a hard time in relationships. Unfortunately, not many were raised in two parent households. Some of us simply don't know how to be in a healthy relationship because we were never taught that at home.

"All right Daddy, next time. You and me, I promise."

"Yeah all right but y'all better be bringing me back something to eat or there won't be a next time. Hold on, here's your mother."

In the background I heard her struggling to get the phone from my dad. He had a tendency to hold full length conversations with people who had originally called to speak to her. Instead, he'd talk for about ten minutes while she tried her best to grab the phone from his hands. They had such a funny routine about them at times.

"Don't mind him Chaka," my mother said as my father still complained about breakfast from a distance. "What's up?"

"Nothing. What time you want to meet?"

"Right now! I'm dressed and ready," she quickly replied.

I looked around my room and grimaced at my unmade bed and dirty clothes all over the floor. There was no way I'd be ready anytime soon. I still needed to shower and get dressed. I hated the fact that my mother was such an early bird.

"Right now Ma? Let me get myself together first, dag. I'll be in front of your building in an hour."

My mother unwillingly agreed. She had probably been awake and ready since the sun came up. She enjoyed our time together and honestly I did too. Our relationship completely changed once she saw me as a woman instead of her little girl.

I wanted to lay back down for a quick thirty minute power nap but I knew if I had done that, I would have never gotten up. It took all of my energy but I finally snapped out of it, made my bed, threw all my clothes into a laundry bag and placed it far enough in the corner so that it was out of sight. Happy to finally see the floor after I removed the heap of clothes, I jumped into the shower.

The water splashed on my body and immediately brought me back to life. I emerged from the bathroom feeling rejuvenated and ready to start my day. I played Biggie Smalls' new CD and blasted the volume all the way up. For a black, fat, ugly nigga, he had a serious swagger about him. I made a mental note to attend his next concert and try to get some backstage access. I wasn't normally attracted to his type but the Notorious BIG, could have gotten some pussy from me at any time.

My outfit for the day was simple – a pair of dark blue Parasuco jeans, a cream cashmere Polo sweater and some brown Gucci sneakers that matched the monogram of my Gucci pocketbook. I pulled my hair into a ponytail and wore my diamond-studded hoop earrings. Even though I was only running routine errands, I had to make sure I still looked good because the streets were always watching.

As I turned the CD off to leave out of the house, I heard someone knocking on the door. I searched my brain trying to remember if I had invited anyone over. I knew my mother would be on her way downstairs and was probably waiting outside for me. I looked through the peephole and almost fainted when I saw Malik's face looking back at me.

I hadn't seen him in a few months so my surprise was expected. The last I heard, he was still sniffing heroin heavy and running around looking like a fiend. Just to make sure I wasn't hallucinating, I looked through the peephole again and yep, it was really him.

I unlocked the top and bottom locks on the door and opened it. The shock of seeing him rendered me speechless. As I looked him up and down, I didn't think he seemed as bad as people in the hood had described him. He had lost a little weight and didn't come off as flossy as he used to be but other than that, he wasn't looking like a train-station panhandler either. He was wearing some construction boots which I could tell were bootleg Timberland knock-offs but they were brand spanking new so he got a pass on that. His jeans were crisp and clean as was his tan Nautica jacket. It was really a *Fraud*itca jacket but who was I to judge? He could've used a shape-up but it wasn't that bad.

"Chako." He smiled and held his arms out toward me. "I can't get no love?"

Hearing my nickname snapped me out of my state of shock. I realized I had been standing there without saying a word.

"Oh, hey, I'm sorry Malik. I mean, damn, this is a surprise," I said while wrapped in his embrace. "Come in."

His scent lingered behind him as he walked into the apartment. He smelled like a mixture of Blue Nile Muslim oil and Irish Spring soap. It wasn't the best combination.

I only allowed him as far as the dining room table before I questioned the reason for his impromptu visit.

"Damn, I gotta have an explanation to come see my young love now?" His tone was polite and heartfelt as it had been in the days when we were together.

Part of my heart still beat for him but my brain was throwing up all types of red flags. Seeing him was like seeing a ghost from my past. Life had changed so much since I was that little girl who constantly bent over backwards for him. But still, I didn't have the power to turn him away.

We talked for about fifteen minutes and in that short time, I noticed there wasn't much that had changed, at least not for him. He had moved back to Brooklyn with his brother, which he claimed was more of a choice than a last option. They were supposedly making a little money but from his fake Timberlands, I knew he was exaggerating about the amount. Denying the drug rumors that were swirling around about him, he assured me that he was still "all good" but needed to get away from everything to get his game back on point. I listened intently without giving much of a response in return. Truthfully, I was still owed some sort of rationale for the whole Far Rockaway bullshit but he didn't bring it up so I didn't either.

"So, I heard my young love got that connect out here now."

He finally revealed the real reason his ass came knocking on my door.

"Who told you that? Niggas be fucking shit all the way up."

"Ain't nobody had to tell me, I just know."

"Well you know wrong because it ain't true."

He sat at the dining room table and looked right through my fabrications. Malik could always tell when I was lying. I noticed his eyes wandering throughout the apartment. It wasn't flashy but there was definitely a sense that somebody with money lived there.

I was getting annoyed with his questions and pretty much with him being there at all. Even though it felt good for him to see how I was living without his sorry ass, I still had things to do and he was just in the way.

"I see I taught you well," he said.

My mouth opened to snap at him for trying to take credit for the things I built on my own but I figured that would have caused a long drawn out conversation and I just wanted him gone.

"Yeah, you taught me a few things." I could sense that he overlooked the patronization coating my words.

He stood up and approached me. I was scared as flashbacks of the many beatings I suffered at his hands flew through my head. My body stiffened as he got closer. But instead of reaching to hit me, he grabbed my shoulders and pulled me to him. I wanted to squirm away but my feet wouldn't move. Forcefully, he shoved his tongue in my mouth. My eyes watered as memories of my love for him overwhelmed me. The tears fell fast while he pulled my sweater over my head and sucked my nipples. My body went limp in his arms.

"You still love me baby," he whispered. "You gonna always love me. You hear that Chaka? I'ma always be inside of you."

I didn't have power over my emotions when it came to Malik and he knew he still had that control over me. Effortlessly, he bent me over the dining room table and slid my pants down. My legs opened as if they had a mind of their own. I came as soon as I felt his dick enter my body.

"Agghh," I gasped while we moved with familiarity. "Oh, Malik I missed you."

It was like my brain had absolutely no dominion over my mouth. I knew being with him, after everything he put me through, was just about the stupidest thing I could have done. Yet somehow, I couldn't stop it from happening. Sexually, he had been the only man to make me feel the way he did. On cue we both stiffened as our bodies prepared to cum, mine for the third time. Together we yelled out in pleasure before he collapsed on my back as I collapsed across the table. Despite all the strength I pretended to have, I was still a love sick weak ass puppy when it came to him.

The phone rang, jolting me out of my shameful daze. He was like dead weight on my back but I somehow managed to nudge him back to consciousness.

"Malik, I have to get the phone," I said and slithered from beneath him.

"Damn, Chak, I forgot how good that shit was."

His lame attempt at a compliment went in one ear and right out the other. I cursed myself for letting him cum inside of me. Somehow, I knew that heat of the moment mistake would one day come back to bite me in the ass.

I got to the phone right before the answering machine picked up. It was Ta-Ta on the other line questioning why I seemed out of breath. I quickly formulated an excuse. There was no way I was admitting that temporary moment of insanity to anybody.

"Girl, I was just about to walk out the door to go meet my mother," I replied loud enough for Malik to hear and get the hint that his ass had already overstayed his welcome.

Ta-Ta spoke in our usual code so nobody could decipher what we were saying over the phone.

"Well, I'm at the doctor's because my foot is still hurting from walking too much. So when I get home, I'm gonna just have to put my feet up for a minute before we go out."

Translated, her words simply meant, "I'm with Manny and I copped a brick. I'm cutting it up now so that when I get home, we just need to bag up and get it ready for pick-up."

"Oh, all right. I'll be back around six so I'll see you then."

When I hung up the phone I realized I had fucked up by announcing exactly what time I was coming back loud enough for Malik to hear. By my count, that was the third mistake I had made since answering the door and allowing him into my apartment. I had to get that nigga the fuck out before I made mistake number four.

I went to the bathroom and wiped myself down with a hot

washcloth. I needed a few seconds to douche his leftovers out of my body but I didn't have enough time to do that and meet my mother. So I just contracted my pussy muscles together real tight and tried to squeeze out any parts of him that remained lodged within my walls. By the time I got back into the living room, he had already poured himself something to drink and sprawled out on my couch.

"Um, I'm about to leave." I was somewhat annoyed that he went into my refrigerator without asking.

"Oh, aight Chako, I'm just gonna wait here for you to get back."

"What?"

Sensing my disapproval, he quickly got defensive. "Oh, you don't want me here?"

"No, I don't. I don't even know why I let you come in anyway."

"Bitch you wouldn't have shit if it wasn't for me. Now you got a little money and you think you all that?" His face went hard in a matter of minutes.

I didn't know how long it was going to take for the real Malik to show up but I knew he would rear his ugly self sooner or later. He picked the remote control up from off of the coffee table and threw it across the room cracking it into pieces. My heart pumped with fear but I didn't move. It was at that moment that I knew regardless of how things turned out, I wasn't going to be afraid of him anymore.

"Can you just leave?" I said without the least bit of desperation.

My words were cold and rigid. There was no need for emotions which would have given him the satisfaction of an argument or a fight. Simply put, I didn't care enough about him for any of that.

Obviously shocked by my detached response, Malik for once, looked defeated. "So that's it, huh?"

"Yup, Malik, I'm done."

He rose to his feet and walked off. My eyes never left the floor. There was no reason to look at him. There was nothing left in him that I wanted to see.

I listened to his footsteps trek beyond the dining room and

halt at the front door. My eyes closed, praying that he would just keep walking.

"You gonna see me again, Chaka," he warned. "That's my word."

And with that, he was gone.

Quickly, I ran and turned all the locks, cursing myself for being so stupid yet again. I stood there for what felt like an eternity until I mustered up enough courage to go outside. Before opening the door, I checked the peephole to make sure he wasn't lurking in the hallway. When I was certain he was gone, I swiftly grabbed my keys and headed out.

I bolted down the stairs as if the Boogie Man was after me. Relief hit me as I stepped out of the building and Malik was nowhere in sight. However, in the back of my mind, I knew then, as I knew when I was a little kid, there was really no escaping the Boogie Man. One day, when you least expected it, he'd come from under your bed and kill you. It was only a matter of time before he'd catch up to you. And in my case, my time was running out faster than I had thought.

CHAPTER 24

My Newport was out by the time I reached my mother who had an aggravated look on her face as I approached. She hated seeing me smoke but after my ordeal with Malik, I needed something to calm my nerves. She also had a thing about being late and by my watch I was already twenty minutes behind schedule.

"Really Chaka?" She spoke before I could even reach her.

Every excuse in the book came to mind but I didn't have the energy to put a good one together so I just told her that I lost track of time. As I got closer, I noticed she was propped up on a walking cane she had in her right hand.

"What's that?" I was puzzled by her new accessory.

"Oh, it's nothing. My legs have been bothering me a little bit. I must be eating too much salt."

I hugged her wanting to ask more about her foot but still too wrapped up in the Malik situation to give it much thought.

We walked, well I walked and she hobbled, to the nearest corner and hopped in an unmarked gypsy cab. The first stop of the day was the Dominicans for a wash and set. Typically, we'd be in and out of the salon in about two hours. But since it was a Saturday and we were already late, as my mother continued to remind me, were weren't surprised to see a line of about ten nappy-headed chicks in front of us. After countless hours of bad ass unruly kids running around, customers arguing with the stylists about their hair not coming out right and stylists talking amongst themselves in Spanish about the chicken head customers who were too bald-headed to be complaining about their hair in the first place, we were finally done and ready to eat. I paid, I tipped and we bounced.

During our salon visit, I noticed my mother wasn't her usual self. Had I not been so consumed with the bull shit I was going through, I would have taken heed to how she seemed to struggle to do even the smallest things like walk from the shampoo sink to the overhead dryer or even get in and out the cab. But being the usual self-centered Chaka that I was, I didn't give it a second thought.

We took a cab to the diner where I immediately delved into one of our regularly scheduled gossip sessions. This routine typically included Taylor but she had chosen to spend her Saturday on a visit with Supreme so I had to fill my mother in on the hood stories by myself. Usually, I could always count on her to engage in an episode of the Queensbridge version of *The Young and the Restless*. However, that lunch date was different. Her mood was aloof and didn't seem at all interested in anything I had to say.

"Ma!" I waved my hands to get her to focus. "Umm, hello, do you not hear me talking to you?"

Clearly she wanted to know the latest "that baby ain't mine" drama. Didn't everybody?

"I'm sorry Chiggy. I just," she paused, "we need to talk."

Her eyes began to well up and I immediately knew that conversation would be one that would stay with me for the rest of my life. I kept quiet, too afraid to hear what she had to say.

"Well," she took a sip of her water, "the real reason I'm using a cane is because my Multiple Sclerosis is back."

The words hit me like a ton of bricks as my eyes darted from her, to the cane that hung from the edge of the table and back to meet her eyes which at that point were full of tears.

"I've been having headaches and so I went to the doctor. They did an MRI and said my brain and spine are full of lesions. The disease is in, what they call a progressive stage now. There's nothing they can do to stop it this time."

Her words were clear but somehow they didn't register. The waiter returned with our food but I was too numb to move my hands. *Multiple Sclerosis*, the words just echoed in my head. I remembered my mother having bouts of the disease when I was younger but it was never anything permanent from what I could recall. Every time she got sick, the doctors gave her some medicine and she always got better. But that word, progressive, just didn't sound good.

"They can't slow it down and they can't stop it from spreading," she said.

"What? What does that mean?"

"It means this right here is probably the healthiest you'll ever see me again. My legs will go soon and I'll need a wheelchair. My eyesight is pretty bad right now as it is. I can't see anything from my left side. It's completely blind."

I couldn't hold the emotions in anymore and let out a scream that caused the whole diner to turn around and look at me.

"Mind your fucking business," I swore to the other patrons who were staring at us.

Normally, I loved being the center of attention yet at that moment, I wanted to seek refuge under a rock where nobody could see me. But like the church hymn says, when God comes knocking, there'll be no hiding place.

"I'm sorry." I made a conscious attempt at lowering my voice. "But why can't they just give you the medicine again?"

"It's not going to help this time, baby."

She reached her hand across the table and held it on top of mine. We sat there in silence both too distraught for words.

"Are you gonna die?" I asked the question despite not really wanting to hear the answer.

"Yes but just not today. So don't go spending all my life insurance money just yet."

Her attempt at light humor didn't go unnoticed. I smiled at her, always the one who somehow managed to make a person laugh through a storm.

We nibbled on our food, neither of us really having the appetite we had when we first arrived. My mother continued to explain the seriousness of her disease. Although I wanted to break down, I knew I had to be strong for her.

I thought back to the first time we learned she was sick. I was in the third grade and woke up to loud screams coming from her bedroom. Without warning, she awoke and was blind in both eyes. After being rushed to the hospital and prodded for numerous tests, we found out that Multiple Sclerosis was the culprit. Before then, nobody in my family had ever heard of that disease.

As a child, it scared me to watch her face balloon from the steroids they gave her to fight off the attack. She confided in me that she missed reading the newspaper. So every day after school, I'd use my little candy money to buy her a Daily News that I would read to her before bed. Whenever we left out, she only trusted me to be by her side. I knew how to hold her hand without looking like I was guiding her. Discreetly, I'd whisper into her ear the name of the person who was approaching us so she could pretend to know who they were when they stopped to talk. She was ashamed to be blind and it was my duty to hide it as well as I could.

There were days when we wouldn't leave the house because of her fear of what people would think. On those bad days, I would sit with her and watch television, describing in full detail what Claire Huxtable was wearing so she'd feel like she could see it with her own eyes.

"Mommy, Claire has on a gold silk dress with pearl earrings and black high heels. And that Rudy, got her hair in those big afro puff ponytails again. But like you told me before, I don't really think that's all her hair though."

Then one day, like magic, she opened her eyes and could see again. The doctors explained that it wasn't really a miracle per se but that her disease had gone into remission. And just like that, life went back to normal.

But this time, as my mother explained, there was no going back to normal. There would be no remission. When her disease came back, it was like the shit came back with a progressively terminal vengeance. She'd get worse and all I could do was slowly watch her deteriorate. The strong beautiful woman, who held it all together for everyone else, would need me to hold it down for her. Unfortunately, I wasn't quite ready for that responsibility.

"Mommy, is there anything I can do?"

Reaching into her purse, she pulled out a pamphlet and passed it to me. I was stumped when I looked at it and read the words United States Navy. She had to know she was too damn old to be thinking about joining the military. Perhaps she wanted me to convince one of my brothers to go.

Sensing my confusion, she announced the pamphlet was actually for me. As she spoke, I nearly choked on my water.

Was she serious? Me? In the fucking military? Yeah right.

After allowing me to catch my breath from her unexpected outburst, she continued. "Look, I can't leave here until I know you're OK. I'm tired Chaka. I don't have the strength to worry about you anymore. If I gotta die, I want to die knowing that you made it out of here. I need to know that all my kids made it out of this trap. I spoke to the people and they said you can get your GED in there. Please just go and see what they're talking about."

"Ma, first of all, you ain't dying. Second of all, I'm getting it together. I don't need to be goi..."

Before I could finish my thought, she pleaded again. "For me baby. Please do it for me."

Reluctantly I agreed, more so because I couldn't stand to see the hurt in her face if I hadn't. Truthfully though, I knew there wasn't a chance in hell I would sign myself up in nobody's Navy. But after all she had been through, I figured a little white lie wouldn't hurt.

We ordered my father's food to go and headed back to her house. She was a little lighter in spirits and I enjoyed seeing her like that. After the day I had, I just wanted to open a bottle of Hennessey and sniff an entire gram of cocaine to numb the pain. But for some reason, I couldn't pull myself away from her.

"Ma, y'all got that new *Pulp Fiction* movie, right?"

"Yeah, your father just bought the bootleg. We were about to watch it tonight so don't even think about borrowing it yet."

"No, I'm coming up to watch it with y'all."

"What? You actually want to hang out with your old mama for once?"

Her smile appeared right away. Regardless of what I did, at the end of the day, I was still her baby.

"Oh whatever." I helped her up the stairs as we entered the building. "Don't get too used to this old lady. When you go into remission, I'm right back out in them streets woman."

She laughed loudly and I knew that I would never forget that sound no matter where life brought me. Before walking through the elevator door, she stopped in front of me and planted a kiss on my lips.

"Yeah but don't think you about to take over the remote control either Missy. Don't let this cane fool you, I'm still the boss of you little girl," she teased as the elevators closed.

"Yes Mommy," I thought to myself, *"and despite how grown I get, that will never change."*

CHAPTER 25

I woke up in a blur not realizing I had fallen asleep with my head on my mother's lap. The last thing I remembered was my father complaining about his fries being cold and my mother telling him to shut up while we were watching the movie. Then, exhaustion got the best of me after my emotional roller coaster of a day and I just knocked out.

"Well good, now that you stopped snoring, maybe we can actually hear the movie," my father said.

"Daddy, I'm a lady. I don't snore. But anyways did Ta-Ta call?" I leaned over the edge of the couch and picked up the house phone to call her.

It was almost eight o'clock when I awoke and I was supposed to meet her at six. Punctuality was never my strong point.

After the phone rang forever, I hung up assuming she probably had the music blasting like she always did. More than likely she was pissed off that I took so long to get home when I knew we had business to handle.

"Dag, y'all shoulda woke me up. I was supposed to be home at six to meet her."

"And there she goes," my mother mumbled under her breath.

"I know, I know, I know. Sorry. Gotta go. Love y'all. Bye." I kissed them goodnight, grabbed my jacket and sprinted out the door.

It was unusually warm out which was good since we were about to hit up some clubs in the city. By the time I reached my building, I had already chosen my outfit for the night in my head. All I had to do was get upstairs, help Ta-Ta finish bagging up if she hadn't done so already, get showered and change my clothes. It wouldn't have taken me more than an hour.

The music was blasting in typical Ta-Ta fashion. When I went to turn the key, I noticed the door wasn't locked.

"Yo, you got the door all open and the music blasting like crazy," I yelled while making sure to lock all the locks and put the chain on the door behind me. "Ta-Ta," I yelled again over the loud music.

When she didn't answer, I figured she was in the back of the apartment, probably getting dressed for the night. She left the scale on the table but there was no product in sight so I knew she had already finished doing what we needed to do. I turned the music down and called out her name again as I made my way to her bedroom.

When I turned the corner from the living room, my heart felt as though it was going to fly out of my chest. There was blood everywhere, on the walls, on the floor, even on the ceiling. And lying face down in a pool of it was Ta-Ta.

Instantaneously, I dove to her side and turned her limp body over only to be more shaken by how she looked from the front. Her shirt was full of blood that continued gushing from her chest even as I tried to clear it from her face so that she could breathe.

"TA-TA, TA-TA, WAKE UP." I grew more frantic by the second. "SOMEBODY, PLEASE HELP ME. OH MY GOD, SOMEBODY."

I heard a muffled moan come out of her mouth. She was still alive.

"Ta-Ta, Oh my God, hold on. Stay awake. I'm not leaving you. I'm here. Ta-Ta, breathe, just breathe."

More moans snapped me into action and I gently laid her back down onto the floor and ran for the phone. All the while I continued to call out to her to hold on.

"911 what is your emergency?"

"Please, my friend is dying. There's blood everywhere. Please hurry. Please. 41-16 Tenth Street, apartment 3B, please, please hurry up."

As soon as I hung up with the 911 Dispatcher, I heard a knock on the door and my neighbor yelling out to me.

"Chaka, Chaka, is everything all right in there?"

She must have heard my screams for help. Quickly I ran to the door and opened it. My neighbor looked petrified when she noticed I was covered in blood.

"Chaka, are you ok? What's going on?"

"Miss Tammy, please help me. It's Ta-Ta, please."

She finally entered the apartment and I ran to Ta-Ta who was still panting and trying her hardest to speak. However, dark burgundy globs of blood were the only thing gurgling from her mouth every time she opened it.

"Ta-Ta, don't say anything," I cried. "Just hold on. The ambulance is coming. They're on the way. You're gonna be ok."

Miss Tammy grabbed a towel and held it firmly against the gaping hole in Ta-Ta's chest. Immediately, I remembered the scale and other shit lying around the house. The last thing I needed was yet another drug-related incident.

"Miss Tammy, I need to get this stuff out of here before the police come. Can you please help me?"

She wasn't really the street type of lady but I had no other choice. She knew my mother and had watched me grow up. Although she didn't agree with my lifestyle, I knew she wasn't going to say no and leave me to fend for myself.

Once she nodded her head in agreement, I let her hold onto Ta-Ta while I started grabbing all the evidence from the kitchen and stuffing it inside a big black plastic bag. The scale, razors, sifters, Pyrex cups, even the glass plate we used to cut up on, all went into the bag so there was no chance of them finding a trace of anything. Unfortunately, the package that Ta-Ta had picked up from Manny was nowhere to be found. I ran through and searched all of our usual hiding spots but kept coming up empty. It had to be gone and chances were, whoever did that to her, also walked away with a few bricks.

Miss Tammy grabbed the bags from my hand and darted to her apartment approximately one second before the ambulance and police arrived at mine. They had to pry me away from Ta-Ta because I was too scared to stop holding her. Everything after that was a blur. I remember the paramedics working furiously to stop her from bleeding out. They cut her clothes off only to reveal even more slashes on her arms, legs and chest. Hazily I answered questions from the police who thought it was appropriate to interrogate me while I was still drenched in my best friend's blood.

"No, I don't know who did this."

"Yes, I found her this way."

"Hell no, I don't know anybody who would have wanted to hurt her."

Though they resisted at first, I was allowed to ride in the ambulance with Ta-Ta. I knew I had to be strong but I couldn't block the flashbacks of the countless cuts and gashes all over her body. I imagined what would have happened had I not fallen asleep at my mother's house. Would I have been able to help her? Or would there have been two bloody rag dolls riding in the ambulance instead of one?

By the time we arrived at the hospital, Ta-Ta's mother and sisters were already there. In my panic, I had forgotten to call them but it didn't matter since news traveled so quickly throughout the hood any fucking way. Reciting the answers to the same questions I had been asked a million times during the brief ambulance ride, my brain felt like it was being hit with a bowling ball over and over again. So many thoughts phased in and out but they all led to the same visions. There was Ta-Ta's lifeless body drowning in a pool of blood and me left standing there, wondering what the fuck happened?

CHAPTER 26

After a few tearful hours, the doctors advised us that Ta-Ta was in critical but stable condition. Though there was a lot of blood, she wasn't stabbed in any major organs. If her body didn't go into shock or succumb to infections, she would likely survive.

In total, she was stabbed seventeen times and would have bled to death had I not arrived when I did. The most serious of the stabs were to her face, exactly a quarter of an inch below her right eye and a cut in her intestines. The latter cut increased the probability of infection. The doctors gave her a 60% chance of making it through the night. It wasn't much but it was all the hope we had.

Before I had time to digest what the doctor said, I looked up and saw my mother wobbling down the hospital corridor toward me with my father right beside her. That was the type of stress she couldn't handle yet there I was forcing her back into my fucked up life. Before they could reach me, I burst into tears and ran into her arms.

I let out a gasp, hoping there wouldn't be another round of questions for which I didn't have the energy or mental capacity to respond

"Mommy." I crumbled, allowing my body to finally give in to the trauma I had just experienced.

"Oh God, you're all right," my mother repeated over and over again.

While she held me, Daddy suggested we go outside and get some air. The stress of the day, combined with the sterile hospital smell and the sounds of the machines they had plugged up to Ta-Ta, pushed me one step closer to complete insanity. So, his suggestion couldn't have come any sooner.

The crisp night air offered a moment of renewal. But no matter how hard I tried, I couldn't get Ta-Ta's face out of my head. She was so broken and simply defenseless. As the sight sent chills down my spine, I clutched the white robe the nurse had given me after arriving in my blood soaked sweater. But still, I felt cold inside.

Damn, I remembered the last time I was there and it was me who was clinging to life. Not even a full year had passed and I was already back. Only that time, it was my best friend knocking on death's door. I knew shit had to change somehow.

Clearly God had other plans for my life, didn't he? I mean, how the fuck did I keep on surviving? Surely it wasn't just so I could fuck up even worse later on down the line, was it?

"Hi Miss Adams." The familiar voice spoke while I waxed philosophical to myself.

I turned to find Detective Salerno standing in front of me still as fine as he was the first time I met him. Coincidentally, it was at that very same hospital.

"Detective Salerno," I nipped with absolutely no interest in yet another round of questioning.

His racist partner was nowhere in sight which gave me some form of relief. The last thing I needed at that point was a know-it-all white cop all up in my area. With my level of frustration being what it was, I would have probably ended up getting arrested for spitting in his face.

"Can I speak to you for a moment, in private?" He nodded his head toward the corner after acknowledging my parents who wouldn't budge.

I let them know I was all right and they walked off to give us some space. However, they stood barely a foot away and strained their necks to hear every word. Throughout the mayhem, they still lived to protect me and that was all the comfort I needed.

"Before you ask, I don't know who did this to her," I said, prior to him uttering what I already knew would be his first question. "I don't know who would have wanted to do this. I don't know what happened. I don't know why it happened. All I know is she was almost dead when I got to her and then I called you."

"We know you weren't there. We spoke to Tamara Roland, your neighbor. She said she heard when you arrived at the apartment and started screaming. But where were you around six o'clock?"

I paused before answering. That was the time I was supposed to meet Ta-Ta at the house. That much I did recall. But how the fuck did he know that?

"Huh? Why are you asking me where I was?"

"I just need to know," he said.

My memory raced back over the day's events. At that point, the hours just seemed to overlap. Too much shit had already gone down for me to remember much of anything.

"Umm, six o'clock, I was at my mother's house. I was sleeping if you must know. Now why did you ask?"

"Because your neighbor said she was coming home from work around six and heard your door slam. It sounded like a little bit of a scuffle but then she reported the music started blaring so she didn't think anything of it. We think whoever did this, entered your apartment around that time."

He continued talking while I scoured my brain to figure out who the fuck would be scuffling in my house.

"Stabbing is a very personal attack usually done by somebody in a hell of a rage. It's not like shooting a person from a distance. She was stabbed seventeen times which leads us to believe she knew her assailant personally and this wasn't a random attack at all."

My insides turned and as he spoke I felt myself getting nauseous. Was it really a personal attack? Who would intentionally want to do that to her? Would they have done the same to me if I was there? The questions formed in my brain one after the other to where I could barely breathe. Suddenly my chest tightened and my heart started beating uncontrollably. I leaned against the brick wall to keep me from passing out.

"Did you notice anything missing when you got there?" He asked.

Hell yeah, like a couple of bricks of uncut cocaine.

Of course I couldn't tell him the truth, so I did what came naturally to me – I lied. "Huh? Was there anything missing? No, there wasn't nothing missing."

"Chaka, I need you to be honest with me. We got a call from an informant who said Malik tried to sell him a large quantity of cocaine today. We've been watching him, we know he doesn't have those types of connections anymore. Word on the street is that you and your friend do. So, I'm going to ask you again, did you notice anything missing when you got there?"

I tried to hold back but it was too late. Before I knew it, vomit flew out of my mouth and splattered all over the concrete. Salerno moved back just in time or it would have landed on him instead. My father grabbed me as I was about to hit the ground.

"That's it, leave her alone. She don't know nothing and she ain't talking to you no more." My mother protectively waved her cane in Salerno's face.

A tremendous wave of panic flashed through my body. My heart was pounding erratically and my chest felt like it was caving in. My breath was short and shallow allowing no air to pump into my lungs. Instantly, I broke into a sweat and felt a numbing sensation initiate from my neck and travel all the way down to my fingertips. Everything started closing in around me and I felt trapped. Had it not been for my father holding me up, my legs would have given out on me.

The day's events vividly reappeared in front of me all at once. Malik overheard me say I was going to be home to meet Ta-Ta at six. He was there when I was on the phone with her. It was me he wanted to hurt, Ta-Ta was just in the wrong place at the wrong time. She was almost killed because of me. Every time I thought about it, I slipped deeper and deeper away from reality. I knew he was going to come back, he warned me of that. I should have told Ta-Ta so she would have been more on-point. The whole shit was my fault.

The realization hit me with a boulder-like force. Somehow I managed to fuck up everything good that came into my life. The closest friend I ever had was one or two stabs away from being just another face on a Rest in Peace t-shirt, all because of me and my bullshit.

From that moment, I realized there was only one way to fix things. And I knew once I did, there would be no turning back.

CHAPTER 27

All the blankets and pillows in the world couldn't have made the chair in the hospital waiting room any more comfortable. But until Ta-Ta made it out of surgery, I wasn't leaving her side. My panic attack saved me from having to endure any more questions from Detective Salerno which was a blessing because I wasn't sure if I could have dodged them much longer anyway.

My parents wanted to bring me back to their apartment for the night but honestly I didn't feel safe anywhere near Queensbridge. While Malik was still roaming the streets, I would have had to watch my back at all times. So once they got me settled down, they left instructions for the hospital to call them immediately if I had another one of those attacks. My mother left looking beyond drained. Dealing with me would only worsen her condition, I was sure of it. I knew shit had to change or I'd bring her to her death much sooner than her Multiple Sclerosis would.

As hours passed and Ta-Ta remained in critical condition, I couldn't do anything but sit and think. My thoughts were schizophrenically roaming from one extreme to the next.

Had I really become this person? What happened to the little girl I used to be? Where was the girl who had dreams of being a lawyer or an author? When I was in the fourth grade, I was already reading college-level books and now the only shit I was reading was The Source magazine. Why hadn't I taken advantage of the full academic scholarship they offered me to attend prep school in Pennsylvania? What was so compelling about Queensbridge that I could never seem to let that place go? Why did I seek out drug-dealer girlfriends to be my role models instead of the quiet nerdy chicks we all laughed at?

The questions seemed to continue without answers. My world was full of excess and that was how I liked it.

However, sitting in a cold hospital forced me to finally take a good look at myself and face the demons I had been running away from for so long. I looked around at Ta-Ta's mother sleeping on the chair beside me. She had been in the streets her whole life. Once a mink-swinging hustler with diamonds, cars and a passport full of stamps, she somehow became an ex-felon just trying to keep her head above water. No more glitz, no more glamour, just a shady past and a hardened heart. There she sat watching her daughter walk the same path and I wondered, years from now, would Ta-Ta and I be doing the same with our daughters?

Thoughts continued to race through my brain making sleep impossible. It wasn't until I saw the sun piercing through the hospital windows that I realized I had been in one spot unmoved for hours.

The doctors entered the waiting room and I didn't know if we should've been jumping for joy or praying to God for mercy. Those heartless motherfuckers always held the same blank facial expression whether they had something good to say or not. Luckily, they told us what we all wanted to hear and the loud sounds of relief were almost deafening.

Ta-Ta had made it through surgery. She lost a lot of blood but they gave her a transfusion to bring her levels back up to normal. Unfortunately, they had to put her in a medically induced coma so that her body would be strong enough to fight off the infections from her ruptured intestine. Even though she wasn't completely stable, the doctors said she'd make it.

Since Ta-Ta was in the clear, the time had come for me to face the reality that waited outside of the hospital. I rented a room at the Marriott near La'Guardia Airport because I was too terrified to go back to Queensbridge. Until I dealt with Malik, I wasn't setting foot into that old apartment. Besides, I wasn't quite ready to see all that blood again. Bad enough, every time I closed my eyes, I was forced to relive the exact moment I found my best friend nearly murdered.

During the ride to the hotel, I made the cab driver stop at The Gap so I could quickly buy something to wear. I grabbed up a t-shirt, gray hoodie and gray sweats. I was thankful my Gucci sneakers were dark leather because the blood was easy to wipe off without staining them too much.

I checked into my room and jumped in the shower. My arms, legs and chest were still covered with Ta-Ta's dried caked up blood. The water turned red as it poured down the drain. Despite just getting my hair done, I still washed it hoping to get the hospital stench out. Everything about me smelled like death so I scrubbed myself until I couldn't smell it anymore.

I knew the next thing I had to do was call Manny. We were supposed to bring him some money that morning so he'd be expecting us to come through as we always did. The Manny call made me nervous. Ta-Ta was usually the one who handled those types of transactions. All I had to do was just sit there and look pretty with a few interesting and witty things to say in between. My heart quickened, forcing me to consciously fight off yet another panic attack and I dialed his number.

"Yo," he answered.

"Hi Manny, umm, this is, umm, Chaka, and umm, I was calling because, umm."

"Yo, where y'all at mamita? Y'all late."

"Umm, well, that's why I'm calling you. See, umm." I still spoke like a fucking Stuttering Stanley. "Yeah umm, what had happened was, umm..."

Immediately he knew something was wrong.

"Nah, not over the phone Mamita. I'm coming to see you. Where are you?"

I hesitated before telling him my location. After all, we

still owed him money and I didn't know if it was a good idea to divulge my whereabouts. On the other hand, I wanted to meet him in a public place rather than venture uptown to his stomping grounds.

Once I told him where I was, he said to give him about thirty minutes to get there which felt like a lifetime. As I paced the room, I wondered how Manny would react if I pretended like I didn't know who robbed us. If he found out about Malik, he would have killed him without question. But if I didn't tell him, then maybe it would have made me look as if the whole shit was set up. I had decisions to make that would be life changing and they all had to be made within thirty fucking minutes.

The knock on the door jolted me into survival mode. Looking through the peephole, I saw Manny who seemed to be alone, which was a good thing. Hesitantly he entered the room, making sure to check both the bathroom and the closet. I guess I wasn't the only one leery at that point. After making sure I was by myself, he sat at the desk and turned his chair to face me. Slowly I exhaled and filled him in on what happened.

He waited until I was done before he said anything. "Damn, but she's gonna make it right?"

I nodded my head in agreement unable to stop myself from choking up a few times while I explained in full detail, all the horrors of the day before.

Manny stayed silent for a minute until he asked the inevitable next question. "Do you know who did this?"

I heard him clearly but once I fully digested not only what he asked but also the consequences of how I would answer, my throat got dry and that damn tingling feeling crept back into my hands and arms. Beads of sweat popped out of my forehead from out of nowhere. The fucking anxiety attacks were making me look like a dopefiend looking for her next hit.

I nodded my head yes but still my tongue felt too paralyzed to move.

Manny, sensing my nervousness, asked again. "Who did this?"

If I answered, I was practically signing Malik's death certificate. But hadn't he already done that on his own?

He almost killed my best friend but in all actuality, that motherfucker really wanted to kill me.

Then reality finally dawned on me like a light bulb being turned on in my head. He didn't give a fuck about me when I was still a wet behind the ears little girl chasing after him and he clearly didn't give a fuck about me when he was ripping that knife through Ta-Ta's flesh. Once I finally accepted the cold hard facts, I knew what I had to do. My only choice was to make him pay for his actions.

Suddenly I was seeking revenge, not only for Ta-Ta, but for every time I cried at the black eyes he gave me, for the times he told me I would never amount to anything without him, for the lessons he taught me on selling drugs instead of pushing me to do something with my life, for making me grow up too quickly into a world where I could no longer believe in happy endings or true love, for ruining me and stealing my innocence all at the same damn time. It was for all of those reasons that I couldn't allow him to live rent-free in my heart anymore. And finally, I had mustered the courage to hate him with every fiber of my being.

"It was Malik," I said with authority. "And I know where you can find him."

My words echoed throughout the room and I knew just what they meant – Malik's death certificate was signed, sealed and soon to be delivered.

CHAPTER 28

As soon as his name rolled across my tongue, I instantly regretted it. However, it was too late. The damage had already been done.

Manny's face filled with rage and his eyes revealed a much darker and sinister side that I had never encountered before then. He knew of Malik from their mutual drug circles but until that moment he hadn't a reason to interact with him whatsoever.

"You fucking that nigga?" His tone was direct and quite matter-of-factly.

"No." I answered quickly, remembering our brief jump-off which eventually resulted in me saying too much in his presence.

"And does he know that's my shit?"

Up until Manny asked that question, I had never really thought about it. But with the hood's loose lips, I realized Malik had to know. After all, he wouldn't have shown up at my crib if he didn't. Even though we thought it was genuine hood love that protected us, the truth of the matter was that Manny was the only thing keeping us safe. Apart from his suave demeanor, he had a Tony Montana reputation on the streets. Simply put, he wasn't the type of motherfucker you wanted to double cross in any sense of the word. His involvement in our empire made the bigger niggas think twice before cutting our throats.

But still Malik didn't seem to give a fuck or maybe he just never thought I'd find out. Perhaps he was that confident that if I did find out, I would never have the heart to tell on him. He was mistaken and would soon discover just how wrong he was.

Manny made a few phone calls. His conversations were in Spanish so I had no idea what the fuck he was saying. Despite the language barrier, there was no mistaking the tone or the purpose of his calls. When he was done on the phone, he instructed me to get my things and leave with him. I was too scared to ask any questions and did exactly as I was told. He didn't seem mad at me but then again I wasn't about to let my slick ass mouth write a check that my ass couldn't cash. So, I shut the fuck up and got into the front passenger seat of his gray Chevy Impala.

"So where is this madigón?" He finally gave me a clue as to what was going on in his head.

Suddenly I went mute. Not only was I about to put him on to Malik but I was also being forced to bring Manny to him. Clearly that thought had never entered my mind. Of course, I knew what was going to happen to Malik but I thought I had done my due diligence once I told Manny who he was and where to find him. My thoughts couldn't have been any further from the truth.

All I could do was face plant into the palms of my outstretched hands and replay all the moves I made in my life that had gotten me to that point. It was like watching a game of chess and I was the overzealous pawn who didn't know how to strategically move across the board. Instead of taking my time, I jumped out unguarded and eager to overthrow the king without much concern of the silent killers who would take my rook down just for shits and giggles.

I shook my head in disbelief. My life, as I had once known it, was over right along with Malik's.

"Look Mamita, I told y'all a long time ago, don't ever cross me. Now this faggot stole my shit. I don't think y'all had nothing to do with that but if you don't help me find him, maybe I'll change my mind and think y'all did. And believe me Chula, you don't wanna know what happens to people that I think are crossing me."

The threat came across loud and clear. It was either my life or Malik's. Without much hesitation or delay, I finally chose me and confessed his whereabouts.

"He's in Brooklyn."

I showed Manny the way and within minutes, we were parked around the corner from his mother's house. From our spot, Manny could still see the front and back doors. Silently I prayed they wouldn't hurt his moms but more selfishly I begged God for them not to hurt me in the process.

His friends pulled up in two more vehicles. One was another Impala and the other looked like a Mexican construction worker's van. It was white and all beat up with no windows except for the driver and passenger side doors. Multi-colored paint streaks spanned from the front wheels all the way to the rear of the van. They parked closer to the house and we waited for what seemed like hours.

Conversation was non-existent between Manny and I. His attention was focused intently on the area surrounding the house. A few times we thought we saw him but each instance was a false alarm. The old saying about us all looking alike was true because every short black dude walking by gave me a near heart-attack until I realized it wasn't Malik.

My mind raced back to Ta-Ta and I wondered if she had gotten any better or any worse. What if she didn't make it and I wasn't there to say goodbye? Then I thought about my mother. How could she handle it if something happened to me? I had no idea if Manny planned on letting me live after he got his hands on Malik. Again, the game of questions was being played so heavily in my head that I almost missed the slight movement across the street. He was dressed in all black from head to toe and lurking deep within the shadows. Right away, I knew it was him.

"There he is." I pointed to the dark sliver crossing the street.

Manny immediately chirped the announcement through his walkie-talkie like telephone. Within seconds, the van doors flung open and two brolic niggas with ski masks jumped out. Their guns were cocked and ready. Malik reached for his waistband but it was too late. Before he could react, he was already bludgeoned with the butt of a gun and yanked up into the van. We followed closely behind as it peeled off. Everything happened so quickly, I don't remember ever hearing a sound.

I wanted to ask where we were going but I was too shell-shocked to speak. The knot in my damn throat made it hard to swallow so I couldn't imagine how difficult it would be to force sound to come out.

We crossed the Pulaski Bridge which led onto the FDR and then across the Third Avenue Bridge. Finally, we arrived at some old abandoned warehouse in The Bronx. The building's bricks looked like they were once white but after years of decay and negligence, they had faded to a dusty gray. The sporadically broken black windows that spanned from one side of the building to the next, blended in with the other vacant buildings grouped together on that desolate industrial block.

The van was already parked and the henchmen with the masks had emerged with Malik. He looked like he could barely stand on his own two feet. From the car, I noticed his face was full of blood like he had been brutally interrogated during the ride across the three boroughs. If he looked that bad already, I hated to think what he would look like once Manny finished with him.

"Let's go." Manny ordered me out of the car.

My legs didn't want to move but I knew I didn't have a choice. Once we stepped into the dark warehouse, I noticed two large Presa Canario dogs, which were more like mutant pit bulls on steroids. They barked like crazy with drool hanging from their mouths as they pulled forcefully on the short leashes attached to the barb-wired collars around their necks. The dude holding them seemed like he was ready to let them go as soon as Manny gave the word.

Malik was seated on a wobbly metal chair in the middle of the room. His arms were tied behind him and his head swerved back and forth, as a result of his neck being too weak to hold it up. Part of me felt heartbroken to see him like that but another part of me took a little pleasure in the sight. He hadn't yet noticed me so I tried to stay hidden in the corner.

Without warning, Manny marched over to him and punched him square in his face. His left cheek exploded on impact once the brass knuckles connected.

"You wanna rob me you fucking faggot," Manny yelled.

"You got the wrong dude. Man, I ain't rob nobody," Malik said.

His denial only infuriated Manny even more as his blows continued more furiously with each punch.

"You gonna lie to my fucking face you black piece of shit? Where the fuck is my shit?"

"I ain't got it. That's my word." Malik's voice whimpered with both pain and fear.

I had never seen him so vulnerable. I winced every time he got hit but there was nothing I could do about it. Everything that transpired was a direct consequence of his own actions.

"Bring me the girl." Manny shouted the order to one of his goons.

I hadn't imagined being brought face to face with Malik. My knees buckled beneath me but I knew I had to move or risk being tied up to a chair right beside him. Malik's face looked surprised at first but then betrayed once he realized the Judas who was selling him out was once the Eve to his Adam. Similarly, my words carried as much weight as her apple and like the hen-pecked Adam, he would have no choice but to swallow them down.

"Come here." Manny motioned for me to stand by his side. "Is this that bitch nigga that took my shit?"

Malik looked at me. His eyes were silently begging for pity. But truth be told, I had none to give. Visions of Ta-Ta tugged at my heart far worse than seeing Malik get what I felt he deserved.

"Yes, that's him." I spoke softly trying to drown out any feelings from my voice. After confirming what was already known, I walked over to Malik and whispered in his ear. "And Ta-Ta is still alive you sorry son of a bitch."

My legs had a mind of their own as one rose up and caught him directly in the chest causing the chair to topple over. Malik tried to wiggle free but he had no luck against the Presa

Canarios, who were already on attack. His screams pierced throughout the warehouse as I watched the crazed animals bite into his flesh ripping chunks of meat right from his body. Manny signaled to stop the dog attack after what appeared to be an appetizer for the beasts in preparation for their main course.

Somehow I managed to squirm my way back into the corner and away from the massacre. If I could have ran out the door, I would have bolted as Manny started walking toward me. But the dude standing guard and holding a big ass shotgun made it impossible for me to escape. Even with my many years of running track, I couldn't outrun a bullet and I wasn't even about to try.

My life flashed in front of me. Right there, alone, in a dark cold warehouse, I had assumed I reached the end of my rope. I wanted to drop to my knees and pray for it to be a quick painless death but I knew after all the shit I had done, I didn't even deserve that much.

"No worries, Chula," Manny said obviously sensing my fear. "I'm not like that puto over there. I won't hurt a woman."

I breathed a sigh of relief but I wouldn't feel completely safe until I was out of there.

"But it's over for you and your friend Ta-Ta. Y'all can't make another dollar in New York mamita. Tu entiende? You're done. This shit is about to get crazy and unless you giving me all the money this punk took from me, it's best for you to leave. If I even hear that you copped a bag, I will find you. Like I said, I don't hurt women but I'm sure some time alone with Primo and Yayo might help you understand." He pointed to the two Presa Canarios as if I needed any additional persuasion.

A shiver went through my body at the thought.

"You got two days to leave New York or I will come find you."

Two days? Where the fuck was I supposed to go? Queensbridge was the only thing I knew.

"There's a driver outside. He'll take you where ever you need to go and remember what I said mamita, two days."

With that, he turned and headed back toward Malik. I, on the other hand, couldn't have run faster in the opposite direction. It felt like I was on my last appeal and the warden decided to issue me a pardon. There was no way I was going to fuck that up.

I reached the door and turned to take one last look at the former shell of the man I once loved. As I did, I saw Manny's outstretched arm with a shiny chrome 44 Magnum handgun pointed between Malik's eyes. For a moment he looked at me and our gaze locked on each other. Undoubtedly, that was going to be our last goodbye. There was really nothing left to say. Our paths had crossed for a reason and only God knew what that reason was.

Time would eventually reveal Malik's purpose in my life but unfortunately for him, time wasn't on his side.

I swung the door open and walked out before I heard the blast.

POW – and just like that, I knew he was gone.

CHAPTER 29

The driver dropped me off at the hospital. Ta-Ta's condition hadn't gotten any better but thankfully it wasn't any worse either. My time was short and I had to say my peace to her before I left. The nurses told me that her mother had just left to go home for a change of clothes but she would be returning soon. It gave me some relief to know that although I wasn't there, Ta-Ta hadn't been completely alone.

Her body was still motionless while machines beeped around her. Once the life of the party, she was now the one who seemed so lifeless.

"Ta-Ta." I collapsed on the chair directly beside her bed. "I'm so sorry."

That might have been the last time I would lay eyes on my best friend or any friend for that matter. The *"Sexy Six"* had already begun to drift in different directions for no other reason than people growing apart. But Ta-Ta was my right hand. She was the Thelma to my Louise. Our bond was supposed to be unbreakable. Besides begging God to protect her, there was nothing else I could do.

I stood and kissed her lips. "Goodbye Ta-Ta, I love you."

Tears overflowed and for once I didn't try to stop them. I needed to let go. A few minutes passed before I headed out of the room. I wanted to stay and hold her hand through everything but Manny made it perfectly clear, I had to get the fuck out of Dodge.

I still wonder if she ever truly forgave me for leaving her side.

The elevator took forever to get to my floor. When it opened, I wished it hadn't once I noticed Detective Salerno standing inside. He grinned when he saw me and didn't bother to exit so I was stuck riding with him down the eleven stories to the lobby.

"Ms. Adams, how are you holding up?"

His tone wasn't condescending or even rude for that matter. On the contrary, he eluded genuine concern.

"How do you think?"

He searched my eyes for non-verbal signals as only a detective could.

"We've been trying to locate Malik to question him about your friend's attack," he said. "Would you happen to know how we can reach him?"

Hearing that name felt like a scalpel scraping across my heart. I shook my head no and shifted my eyes back down to the floor. They were the windows to my truth and I intended on taking the Malik situation to the grave with me.

The doors to the elevator couldn't have opened any sooner. I scurried past him and almost made it out of the hospital doors before he called out to me.

"Ms. Adams, I was wondering if you had given any thought to that Navy opportunity."

His question stopped me dead in my tracks. *How the fuck did he know about the Navy?*

"I'm the one who sent your mother the information about it," he said.

"You did what?"

We had both exited the hospital although I felt like I was walking on a cloud of confusion.

"Look, I've watched you for a long time. I know your past. I know where you are now. But what I don't understand is why you choose to stay like this. Some people don't have a choice, this is all they know. But you're different."

His words baffled me. Why the fuck did he care? He was after something, I knew it. In my world, there were always ulterior motives.

Sensing my skepticism, he went on. "I wasn't always a cop Ms. Adams. I was just like you once. I was a kid growing up in the projects on the Lower East Side. The only difference was that I was a white kid trying to fit in so you could imagine how much harder it was for me."

Who would have thought Detective Salerno was a project kid from dirty ass L.E.S. of all places?

"Look," he continued, "all I'm saying is the military was my one shot to get my life back on track. And if I'm being honest, it's your only shot. You remind me a lot of my sister. She also chased the streets until one day the streets caught up to her. I couldn't help her, nobody could. But I'm trying to help you. I know the recruiter and he said he spoke to your mother. I know she's sick. Don't let her die thinking you never made it out of there."

The thought of losing my mother weighed heavily on my heart. Salerno knew all the right strings to pull too. All I had done was hurt her with disappointments and fuck-ups. She once had the highest hopes for me. I was her pretty little smart girl who she loved more than she loved herself.

A mother's love is eternally blind.

I knew I had to change. I had to make it up to her for all those sleepless nights she lied awake crying for me. For every door she knocked on looking for me when I didn't come home some nights. Even if it was only for the short time she had left, I had to make her proud.

"The recruiter also said they have space immediately. I can make a call and you can leave tomorrow morning," he said.

"Tomorrow?"

Inhaling deeply, I realized the time had finally come for me to grow up and really be the woman I kept pretending to be. I had to leave New York anyway so why not leave and do something better with my life?

"Can I say goodbye to my family first?"

Detective Salerno smiled. For the first time in a long time, it made me feel as if I had made someone proud of me. It had been years since I had that feeling.

"Yes, of course you can see your family first. I'll have the recruiter be at your mother's house at six in the morning. Don't worry, if you can survive this hell hole, you can survive Boot Camp."

"Thank you." I silently mouthed the words to him before jumping into the cab that was parked in front of the hospital.

I rode back to the projects, completely amazed by the recent turn of events. Even more so, I was astonished that my fairy godmother would come into my life disguised as a sexy ass white cop from the Lower East Side.

Thinking back, Disney never prepared me for that in any of their story books.

CHAPTER 30

The recruiter had already contacted my parents by the time I reached their house. Genuine happiness exuded from the smiles on their faces. Taylor was also there along with my two brothers. We forced my father to finally pop the bottle of Moët he'd been saving since I was a kid. I couldn't believe they were all celebrating for me.

It felt good to laugh and reminisce about the old days when we'd walk across the 59th Street Bridge singing along to Motown songs. My brothers would be holding my mother's hands while I sat on top of Daddy's shoulders. Regrettably, for so long, my family had come second to the street life that I craved. We were once such a tight unit and I knew getting my life together would be the first brick I laid toward rebuilding it.

I looked around at my brothers, both of whom were in high school. The oldest one was about to graduate and go to College. Even Taylor had found a job as a receptionist in some Manhattan law firm. It dawned on me that although I was once viewed as the child with the most promise, I had become the black sheep. There I thought I was the shit with my fast money, foreign bags and fly lifestyle. But in fact, I was just a nobody who had nothing. They were truly the ones who were successful, not me.

We stayed awake talking and laughing until the sun came up. Right at six sharp, the phone rang. The recruiter was already downstairs parked in front of the building. I grabbed my small bag stocked with toiletries and necessities I figured I would need. The realization that I was leaving left me wrought with emotions. I was finally on my way to do something we all knew would be better than what I had been doing for way too long. Our tears were full of joy and relief after what had been the most defining year of my life.

Funny, I've been trying for almost twenty years to fix a life that only took me one year to fuck up.

My brothers, who normally shied away from girly emotions, embraced me with pride. Taylor, who was such an emotional rollercoaster anyway, couldn't verbalize her thoughts but through her watery hazel eyes I knew what she wanted to say. My departure symbolized everything she wanted to do with her life but just didn't know how to climb out of the barrel. Through me, she was able to make her wrongs right again.

I took one more look around the two bedroom fourth floor apartment and realized just how small it was. I had outgrown the box that was once my entire world.

"Come on baby." My mother rubbed my back sensing the foreseeable breakdown. "It's time to go."

As we emerged from the building, I noticed my father held his head a little higher than usual. His former street-bound, high school dropout, cokehead of a daughter was taking the first step toward completely changing her life.

He wrapped his arms around my neck while we walked to the car. "I'm proud of you Chiggy. Now get over there and do the damn thing."

I stopped and held my father tightly feeling once again like his little girl.

"Thank you Daddy. I love you and I'm sorry."

We held each other for a while until we both felt strong enough to let go.

I still haven't felt arms more comforting than my Daddy's.

The recruiter, dressed in a Navy uniform, opened the car door as we approached.

My mother stood in front of me revived with a glow of promise and said, "Chaka, this is your gift from God, don't waste it baby girl. There's something inside of you that he wants the world to see. When you were a kid you always said you wanted to be just like me when you grew up. But baby, I don't want you to be anything like me. I want you to be better than I ever was. I've never been more proud of you than I am right now."

Finally, the onslaught of feelings I had been holding in took over and I dissolved into my mother's hug. "I love you and I promise, I'm gonna make it Mommy. I'm gonna make it."

Rigidly interrupting, the recruiter asked, "You ready to start a new chapter Seaman Recruit Adams?"

The name he called me was different but I would have to get used to it. That was who I was about to become. It was funny that a girl who let semen change her world was now being referred to as a Seaman – *but that's a whole other type of book.*

My parents gave me one last farewell hug and just like that I was ready to go. I glanced across the street and saw Detective Salerno sitting in a parked car. He waved and flashed that sly sexy smirk of his that I had grown to like. He thought he was parked discreetly but unbeknownst to him, I checked outside the window every thirty minutes out of both paranoia and wanting to make sure he was still there. And he was. He remained parked in the same place and had not moved an inch.

I would never know Salerno's reasons for protecting me until much later on in my life when our roles switched and his survival rested in my hands. But at that moment, he too had come to see me off.

In spite of it all, there were still people who believed in me and I knew I would spend my life making sure I didn't let any of them down.

The car drove off and I locked eyes with my parents until I couldn't see them anymore. As we crossed over the 59th

Street Bridge, which towered the projects and offered a full aerial view, I watched as the six blocks and ninety-six rooftops morphed into a maze before me. It was easy to enter but harder than a motherfucker to get out. For some more than others, it's a lot tougher to crawl their way atop of that barrel. But I was that one tenacious crab who actually did make it out and I was determined to stay out until something forced me to go back.

Unfortunately for me, the Big Apple would come calling and Queensbridge would once again be at its rotten core. And that something forcing me back would come a lot sooner than I had hoped.

Turn the page for a preview of the next installment in the "View" trilogy...

A View of The Bottom

Excerpt

Queensbridge 1981
"You make me sick. I can't stand you, stupid," I yelled at my brother as he grabbed the cheese from my hand. "Watch when Mommy get back out here, you gonna be in trouble."

My brothers made it a habit to make my life a living hell, especially when Mommy and Daddy were in the bathroom doing "grown folk stuff". Well, that's what they called it anyway.

I looked in the refrigerator and prayed that some kind of food would have magically appeared since the last time I checked. Despite the fact that my mother had just gotten her food stamps three hours before, it didn't seem like we were going food shopping anytime soon. So, just as I expected, besides the half-empty bottle of ketchup, there wasn't anything in there to eat except that government issued welfare food.

Of course if I was starving like an Ethiopian, I could have had some powdered milk that was so thick and full of lumps, I practically had to chew it to get it down my throat. Surely, I could have broken off a piece of the gigantic blocks of butter that were accumulating as part of the bench-dweller's trade, *"I'll give you a block of butter for a bottle of your honey."*

I never liked any of the surplus scraps they gave us. First of all, it was embarrassing as fuck to have to stand on that welfare line waiting for the church to open to pick up your family's USDA food ration. What was even worse was when you had a conniving ass mother who made you stand in line for every member of your family who had a Welfare Benefits card. I'd be in line and my brother would be standing about ten people behind me, followed by my sister who was like four or five people behind him. Luckily our last name was Adams and since it started with the letter "A" and rations were distributed by your last name, we were in and out of there with the quickness.

Shit, I would have hated to be a Williams.

As soon as we got the food to our apartment, I went straight to the only thing I did like – my weakness was the cheese. The highlight of the semi-annual food distribution was undoubtedly the cheese. They gave us a big block, like the ones they have at the deli. The only thing wrong with that bright idea was the shit wasn't sliced. Since nobody had a fancy deli-style slicer in the hood, we just had to get ill with a knife and cut it straight enough so that it looked better than some plastic-wrapped Velveeta. In reality it looked more like a jagged glob of hardened yellow clay but when you're dirt poor, you learn to use your imagination to see shit the way you wished it to be instead of the way it really was.

It came wrapped in plastic inside of a brown cardboard box with the letters USDA boldly stamped all over it – as if they weren't going to let you hide the fact that you were getting government assistance. My mother had them fooled though. She would take it out of the box, that lacked a listing of ingredients or an expiration date, and put it in a Tupperware bowl instead.

So when my brother grabbed the last piece as I was stabbing my dull butter knife through the block, I could have killed him. He knew I wouldn't eat that other shit.

"Ma, he took my cheese." I banged on the bathroom door. My parents had been in there for well over an hour.

"All right baby, I'm coming. Me and your father is just talking," she yelled through the wooden door.

I stood there tapping my foot hoping that she would get the

hint and come out. She didn't.

Instead, she yelled even louder. "Chaka, get the fuck away from that god damn door right now before I come out there. I said I'm coming out in a minute. Now, go sit yo' ass in that motherfucking living room before we don't go food shopping or no god damn where."

I stubbornly stood there, folded my arms and started humming loud enough for her to realize that I wasn't going anywhere. If she wanted me to move, she was going to have to finally come out of the bathroom and make me.

"We coming Chiggy Wiggy," my father coaxed, still through the door.

Whenever they were doing "grown folks stuff", he was always the sweeter of the two.

"All right Daddy but hurry up because they keep bothering me," I whined to my father who was a sucker for his little princess.

"What did I say?" my mother hissed. "Now go on, I'm doing grown folks stuff right now. And I said I'm coming."

"Urrggghhh," I groaned before nearly sucking my teeth down my throat and loudly stomping off in a hissy fit.

I stormed over to the wooden RCA Hi-Fi radio, that was already tuned to WBLS, and blasted Chaka Khan's *"What Cha' Gonna Do For Me"* from the speakers. The volume was turned up as loud as it would go. If nothing else was going to make my mother come out of the bathroom, I knew that would. I was ready to get a beating if it meant we could finally go get something to eat.

"You always tryna get somebody in trouble, here." My brother finally passed me the cheese.

As always, a little temper tantrum never hurt nobody.

I smirked at my brothers, one who was only ten months older than me and the other who was still in his walker. We had a sister and brother in between us but they had already been taken away by Child Protective Services. I had never known the truth but I heard it had something to do with them being born with heroin in their system or some shit like that.

Luckily, my mother snuck out of the hospital before they checked us for drugs. Had she stayed any longer, we would have been in foster care right along with them.

My older brother and I didn't have the same biological mother or father. But, my mother was a mother to him and his father was a father to me so we were brother and sister. We never referred to that half-brother, step-sister shit. If we had to grind together, we were blood.

We had sisters who were about seven years older than us. With so many years in between, they were already into their own things by then and were barely in the house.

I chomped on my cheese while my little brother kept banging his walker into the wall. He'd bounce off, start laughing and then bang into it again. In my opinion, that shit looked retarded. I mean, why keep banging into the same wall over and over again? Where's the fun in that?

BAM

I immediately turned toward my brother thinking he broke something in the living room which was going to get us all an ass whooping. But my mother's thunderous shrieks from the back of the apartment forced my attention elsewhere. Whatever made that loud sound was a lot worse than anything my brother could have done.

I hopped off of the wooden Hi-Fi stereo and ran to the bathroom. Before I could fully get around the corner and beyond the hallway closet, I saw my father sprawled out on the floor. Remembering that my brothers were right behind me, I tried my hardest to push the little one away before he could see it too. But it was too late – we were all there looking at Daddy with a syringe still stuck in his arm and white foam spouting from his mouth. My mother, in a hysterical fit, couldn't stop yelling.

"FREDDY, GET UP," she screamed. "FREDDY."

Daddy didn't budge and neither did my mother except to smack his face continually as she called out his name. My older brother immediately ran into the room and cowered shakingly in the corner, while my little brother started screaming at the top of his lungs trying to pull his walker through the narrow hallway leading to the bathroom. As for me, I just stood there shocked and too afraid to move.

"CHAKA, CHAKA, GO GET SOME ICE," my mother ordered.

I heard her but my feet stayed planted.

"GOD DAMNIT CHAKA, GO GET SOME GOD DAMN ICE FOR YOUR FATHER. GO, HURRY UP."

The second time she said it, I went into action. I practically had to jump over my brother's walker, toppling him in the process, and dash to the refrigerator. I opened the freezer and grabbed two ice trays and a bag of frozen peas. I would have grabbed more but that was the only shit in there. By the time I got back to my father, my mother had already stripped him to his underwear. So not only did I have to watch him having an overdose with a needle still stuck in his arm but I also had to see him half naked.

While my mother kept calling out his name, my little brother furiously wailed and my older brother stayed hidden in our room. I just stood there holding two ice trays and a bag of no-frills peas from Pathmark.

"COME PUT THE ICE ON HIS CHEST, CHAKA," my mother yelled out to me.

My body moved on its own as I jumped to Daddy's side and started rubbing the ice on his chest. Every time my mother yelled, I tried to yell much louder.

"DADDY, GET UP. DADDY, DADDDDDDY."

"CHAKA, PUT THEM PEAS IN HIS UNDERWEAR."

What? Did she really want me putting my hands down Daddy's draws?

My hesitation lasted too long because my mother grabbed the peas and smacked me across the face with them.

"PUT IT DOWN HIS DAMN DRAWS RIGHT NOW CHAKA. I AIN'T PLAYING WITH YOU," she warned before turning back to rub ice on my father's neck and face. "FREDDY COME ON MAN, DON'T LEAVE ME."

I closed my eyes, pulled the elastic from the waistband

of Daddy's underwear and shoved the peas down. Quickly, I pulled my hand back and continued yelling his name as I spread the now melting ice all over his legs.

In my five-year-old mind, the whole ordeal went on for hours. In reality, it took about three minutes for my father to start snapping out of it.

"DADDY," I squealed once he started coughing and opening his eyes.

My mother sat him up against the closet door and repeatedly slapped his cheeks to get him to focus. When he did, I heard him whisper to her, "Deb, we gotta go get some more of that shit right there."

———————————

My body jerked as I fought to awaken myself from that nightmare. I hated the flashbacks that crept into my thoughts more and more frequently. Panting wildly, I looked around to make sure it was just a dream. I only calmed down once I glanced over at Jamere, who was peacefully sleeping next to me. I rubbed my belly and said a silent prayer to never let my child go through that type of shit. No matter what I had to do, she was never going to endure one moment of the fear that haunted my memories.

"What's the matter baby?" Jamere slowly sat up and wrapped his arms around me from behind.

"Nothing, I just can't sleep. I can't get comfortable with this big old stomach."

"Hey, watch ya' mouth. You talking about my baby's big old head in that stomach," he said as he kissed my six months pregnant bump.

Jamere always had a way of making me smile. Before I moved down to Atlanta, I would have never thought that we would be having a baby girl and getting married in a few months. Shit has a way of being right in front of you but so far from your sight.

"Come on babe, lay back down. I'll tell you a bedtime story little girl."

"Whatever, fuck you and your story. Just rub my back."

I settled back down while Jamere's hands soothed me to sleep. Had it not been for the slight crack of the staircase leading to our room, I would have stayed in la-la land. But before I could react to the sound, the bedroom door had already flung open.

"You bitch ass motherfucker, get the fuck on the floor," said the voice coming from the person standing before me who was dressed in all black.

It felt like I was watching a movie as Jamere's body was hauled off the bed in slow motion.

"JAMERE," I yelled out before the hand grabbed my jaw and pointed the barrel in my mouth. I felt my front tooth chip as it collided with the gun.

"Oh you thought I wasn't gonna catch up to you, huh, bitch?"

My eyes sprung open at the sight of the ghost from my past.

How the fuck did he find out where I was?

From the corner of my eye, I saw Jamere jump up and try to ambush the dude that held me captive on the bed. But what he couldn't see was the other guy coming from behind the dark shadows of the bedroom door. His gun was already drawn and aimed right at the back of Jamere's head. I wanted to warn him but the gat was so far down my throat that I could barely fucking breathe. As I watched the dude with his outstretched arm, slither closer to Jamere, I looked back up at my gunman in disbelief.

Damn, I knew he was gonna come back sooner or later. I just didn't think this nigga was coming back so strong.

POW.....